THE TRAVELLER.

Garrett Addison

ISBN-10: 0987509152

ISBN-13: 978-0-9875091-5-4

DEDICATION

For my family.

Chapter - 1.

"How long's this one for?" my wife asked with an ambiguous level of interest while I threw my 'A' set of clothes into my usual red suitcase. I cringed and fought to compose myself at that question, familiar and inevitable. Whether it's going to be a long one or just an overnighter any reply I give is equally likely to be received with ambivalence or resentment, so I naturally tried to change the direction of the pending argument, "Not long. I'll be back in time for …". I couldn't for the life of me remember what I was to miss on this particular occasion. This wasn't good grounds for me to field the query.

Surprisingly though, my wife was very accommodating and didn't seize the gift of an opportunity to win another round of our perpetual row. "This trip won't be like the others," she said.

"I can't not go," I groaned, choosing to cautiously deal with her comment as if a pre-cursor to the familiar 'don't go' themed discussion. "You know what the Anti-Christ will think."

"I know you have to go," she said with heartfelt understanding. "I'm just saying this one will be different." My comment didn't even incite a reference to my boss.

"I sincerely doubt it," I mumbled and was even tempted to ask her to qualify what she meant, but I didn't. "It's going to be the same crap." In this case, she would have been right, but to challenge her was to provoke the typical discord or invite an explanation of her fey perception, both of which never end well. It's just like hearing what I missed each time I come home, good and bad, and how the family coped, even though whether they managed well or poorly is very much like debating my favourite between gonorrhoea and syphilis. Then the arguments always start. 'So when are you going away again?'. It's either too soon or not soon enough. On this occasion she let it go and didn't say anything.

"It's not like I want to go," I continued, softening my approach when I didn't get any reaction. She's many frequent flyer miles short of the epiphany beyond the great myth of work travel when the novelty value passes, despite my perpetual efforts to convince her otherwise. After crossing that line initially so many years ago and so routinely since, to me the travel is just the mundane punctuation between visits home and the myriad of different companies I consult to. There's no fun or excitement in it; it's just something I need to contend with and tolerate unless I want to look elsewhere for employment. Today she only shrugged and smiled, stroking one of the many business shirts in my case which she'd purchased for me over the years.

That she was so calm on the cusp of another of my departures un-nerved me and again tempted me to segue our discussion as a distraction to my packing. The 'Anti-Christ', otherwise known as my boss and the reason why I don't leave my job is a familiar theme and often ends in us ranting over the one who presides over the perpetual blur between my personal and professional lives. Then I anticipated the way that exchange would go and I went cold on the idea. My wife would inevitably tell me to look for another job like she normally did and while she has a point, I always resented her suggesting it as if I hadn't considered it myself. I consider it every single day.

"See how you feel after this one," she said. No provocation, no anger, no resentment, no resignation, no frustration. My wife never baulked at any excuse to say what she thinks of my boss or my travel, but on this occasion she did. My wife knows how my boss's absolute power renders me fearful, docile, not really ever at home and travelling so widely that I'm rarely in the same city or country more than a few times. In particular, my wife sees my struggle to find balance and the incessant failure in my eyes each day I come home defeated. It was wholly unlike her to not at least comment on what she thought of my fielding the abusive calls from my boss day and night, or that there are voids in our time together at the dubious whims of a manager with all the human qualities of a virus. I gathered our last hours together were not going to degrade into well-meaning discussion of my options; something I was particularly thankful for.

Then my wife caught me from left field with what epitomised her 'cup half full' biased interpretation of my travelling life. "This trip will be different. Just embrace it," she said, throwing her idea of a lucky tie into my case for good measure just before I closed it. The remark did not go un-noticed though.

I took my case to the door and thought about her frustrating optimism, often a precursor to banter illustrating how little she really understands my travelling life. Somehow she's remained oblivious to the jetlagged sleep deprivation, long days working like a seal weary from the matinee but still performing for the afternoon and evening shows, and often obligatory socialisation in accordance with cultural or professional expectations. When I'm not being coerced into long hours of pseudo-social drinking, I'm alone in my hotel room, alone at a bar or alone at a restaurant for dinner. The next day it all starts again. The destinations change, but the routine is always the same. All this and still subject to derision by phone, email or my boss's favourite: professional malignment by third party.

Then this particular trip assumed a familiar feel despite my wife's initial foreboding and aloof behaviour. "Off you go then, again," she said. The turn in her mood had come a little later than usual, but there it was, cold and angry. "We'll be ok. Again." It was the usual seed for an argument narrowly averted by the arrival of my taxi. My wife's parting words as I left were a shot, a suggestion my trip was little more than a sexual rendezvous with 'Stalin', another less than flattering pet-name for my boss.

I settled into my routine for my 'red-eye', the mid-night flight designed for the desperate or those naively trying to maximise their at-home time. Falling into the latter category, I'd chosen the flight deliberately and to me it epitomised my best efforts in trying for a work-life balance. It also saved me from having to contend with sad farewells from disappointed children in favour of just not being there in the morning when they woke. After a few beers at the airport lounge, I switched to cheap scotch as soon as I was airborne and the free alcohol of the international flight started to flow, occasionally adding a 'Virgin Mary' to demonstrate my commitment to hydration. The air hostess and I both knew the tomato juice was just a ruse to keep the liquor flowing, but she conceded nothing.

As my blood alcohol level rose, my mood mellowed and I settled to watch an impressive electrical storm through the aircraft window. The fingers of light enveloped the entire fuselage and while no-one spoke to me, clearly most passengers were concerned as to whether the plane really was as safe as the captain insisted amid the perpetual vibrations of thunder. Despite being more than a little un-nerved, I didn't share the abject fear of others. After having lived so long in fear at work I wasn't worried for whether I lived or died. For this I held my boss responsible, the one who had systematically destroyed my confidence and will over the years and to such an extent that I was now just a drone at her bidding. Castration by wayward lightning strike would not have taken anything from me she hadn't taken already. Between the near perpetual travel and her abusive inspiration she'd all but killed me inside, so in contrast the lightning really wasn't that big a deal.

Eventually the liquor began to sedate me a little, though not quickly enough to prevent me spilling some juice over myself before I nodded off. The hostess made some attempt to sponge me clean while I probably made drunken small-talk and wondered if there was something even remotely sexual in her attentiveness to my lap. God knows what I said to her. By this time I was barely coherent to myself so I don't think I would have presented myself well to anyone, her in particular.

Chapter - 2.

I remember rousing some hours later to the first hint of dawn over the starboard wing and the smells of day-old bacon, re-constituted scrambled eggs and bitter coffee, all of which appealed, and I had no hangover. I should have known something was different immediately. The hostess, my hostess, even shared a smile better suited to first class while she offered me more than my share of juice and I accepted graciously and as politely as I could. Perhaps I would have made some sober, clever remark or made an attempt to be more than a humble economy class guest if I'd remembered her name from the evening before.

I met up with her again going through the arrivals hall. Priority baggage handling, my company's best effort in-lieu of an upgrade, had me quickly through proceedings, though nowhere near as quickly as all of the aircrew. She watched me get into a discussion with an immigration official about the validity of my visa, smiling with empathy at the posturing of the official in his moment of power. Out of the terminal, she separated from her colleagues as they headed to a staff minibus while she grabbed a taxi. She knew I was watching her and she waited with the taxi door open suggestively.

I stared at her for a time; I couldn't help it. I'd smelled her on the plane; all freshly scented when everyone else was an ambiguous mix of odours and hygiene routines interrupted by travel. Her airline uniform was shapely and beyond merely tailored to fit. Unlike the other hostesses who really only looked like they were wearing a uniform, she looked as if she was dressed to impress. I'd fought the temptation to admire her breasts as she'd leaned over me to deliver my on-board meals, but I hadn't previously noticed her eyes. Now those eyes beckoned me with a bewitching sexuality. Entranced, I made a bee-line for her in the back seat of the cab.

Her name was Faye, 'Fanny' to her friends. Now sober enough to resist any quips at her nickname, I didn't repel her advances. The clichés of sexual fire amongst the service industry, including as it seemed air hostesses, were well founded. The kissing and petting started immediately, and I was appreciative for my previously arranged express check-in at the hotel. Without it I was liable to violate local laws intended to ensure some levels of common decency were maintained.

Sex was imminent; we both knew it and craved it. We managed to walk calmly to my room but once inside we shed our clothes recklessly and cast them where they lay. We fell to the bed and began to savage each other in some pre-penetration foreplay which lasted longer than seemed reasonable and realistic. I savoured the feel, the smell and the taste of her until the outside world beckoned.

The porter might have been knocking or waiting at the door for some time but I didn't notice; I was too engrossed. Then I suddenly noticed the simultaneous rings of the room phone, my own phone ringing from somewhere amid my clothing strewn on the floor between the door and the bed, and the polite persistence of the porter. He could have just left the suitcase, but clearly he wanted his tip or perhaps a look at what I was getting, based on the noises which must have been evident from the corridor.

I remember feeling strangely conflicted and stressed at the need to deal with the phones and to quickly get a grip on reality. Now an hour late for my 8am meeting, people weren't pleased. That the timing of that engagement given my flight's arrival was always going to be a stretch, even without my sordid dalliance, did not rate a mention and certainly wasn't going to mitigate any lateness on my part.

I answered the phones reluctantly but didn't bother to defend myself, offer any excuses or lie that my flight had been delayed. They wouldn't care, and for all I knew whoever had put the call directly through to my room may well have let it slip that I'd checked-in some time ago and surely I'd had enough time to shower and change. I didn't even shave, just re-dressed in the same dirty clothes I'd travelled in leaving Fanny reclining on my bed, fully expectant she wouldn't be there on my return.

When I saw myself in a mirror in the lift to the lobby, I was surprised. My clothes clearly had a lived-in look about them and I looked very much like someone who had travelled overnight, sleeping in the same clothes. If my sense of smell wasn't still temporarily shot from the dry pressurised air of the aircraft cabin, perhaps I might have smelled like a mix of alcohol and bodily fluids, but I didn't dwell on it. Instead, I focused on the way I presented myself. Beyond my dishevelled state, I liked what I saw.

Whether I could attribute how I looked to fatigue, stress or my long bottled indifference to my work and associated travel I'll never know, but I didn't see a messy, hung over, adulterous, struggling professional who was running late. Instead, I saw a man, brimming with such self confidence that he didn't need to waste any time on the mundanities of his life. This man was going to make those at the meeting wait because they ought to, and doing so allowed them time to contemplate the understated value of him. There was a presence about this man, an arrogance born of capability; he could do anything. It took me a while to acknowledge that this man, this man exuding power, was me.

I didn't rush to the meeting. My phone rang incessantly but I just let it ring and I settled myself for a decent coffee before casually hailing a cab for the short four block hop. Coffee in hand and surrounded by the City's hum, I anticipated my morning motivational call from my boss and thought about whether the presence of this man from the mirror would support me when she abused me for any or all of my many failings. When she didn't ring I wondered if the man from the mirror ever worried.

I wondered for a time if my clients saw what I did when I strutted across the lobby of their conference room. They talked among themselves as I approached and I sensed their aggravation, unimpressed that a consultant for whom they were paying a fortune would keep them waiting, but before they could say anything something came over me and I brazenly launched into an assault on them, "Care to tell me why you won't let me finish my coffee in peace?".

They looked at each other with a look of bewilderment that transcended our cultural divides. "I'll start when I'm ready," I scolded, labouring the point while they were taken aback. They were silenced by my front and the mood eased a little, but something in the back of my mind wondered whether my façade would withstand any committed scrutiny.

They escorted me to a vacant desk with some reluctance while an interpreter reiterated my brief and what they expected me to achieve, adding a little quip that I should try to work 'full' days if it wasn't too much trouble. Resting my jacket on the back of my chair, I settled in for the familiar tedium of another day of picking holes in the way the company operated until I caught another glimpse of my reflection on the screen. A different person looked back at me; I could see it in everything about me. There was a bizarre fluidity in way I moved, there was acuity in my thinking and each breath from me felt like it was clean exhaust from a fusion reactor. Attributing this person to the result of tired eyes, I rubbed my face and when I looked again I only saw myself.

I set to work until my mind drifted a little. I thought of how my contacts had seemed good humoured, particularly with my professional arrogance, but then I felt as if this was just a passive friendly air and a darker more militant reaction was in the winds. On several occasions my mind tricked me into feeling the vibration of an incoming call, but on looking my phone showed no sign of anything, missed or pending. This was surely a bad sign, most probably that my boss was en-route to deal with me personally, and these affable clients were just biding their time before ultimately they'd have the last laugh. Taking travel time into consideration I figured I might well need to wait until the following morning before I could really be sure if my concerns were warranted.

Despite being fuelled by my potential, I found myself driven partially by obligation to perform and stress for consequences of failure and how my boss would respond and my initial tardiness. Focussing on the task at hand, it was as if the planets came into alignment as I became a man apart. By early afternoon I'd finished what I'd travelled many frequent flyer miles to achieve. What had been estimated to take two weeks, and not by any miscalculation, deliberate or otherwise, I had completed in a little over four hours. As I worked I felt the presence of regular employees, mere ordinary mortals, come and go, each looking over my shoulder to watch me work. They watched the blur of my hands over the keyboard and the incessant flashes of productivity evidenced on the screen and shook their heads in disbelief. The clients were in awe, and I was more than a little impressed with my achievement too. Soon I was doing little more than housekeeping, wiping dust from the desk and ordering the selection of stationery in the drawers. Frustrated at being in a position I didn't recall ever having been in before, I found some paperwork to complete and then made a list of everything else which could be done while on-site; the 'as opportunity' tasks for which I never got an opportunity. Then I completed everything on the list.

Admittedly, I was in Asia, but I was surprised when one of the heavy hitters in the client organisation bowed his head slowly when he had some occasion to visit. He had clearly been well briefed on what I had achieved and perhaps he came to see for himself. His entourage was large which, correctly or not, emphasised his importance to them if not to me. As buoyed as my spirits were, it was possible I could have misinterpreted a neck flinch as a subtle bow, but there was no mistaking the exaggerated almost cowering bow of his followers. *En masse* their conduct made me feel like I was royalty.

Far from discounting their praise or similarly deriding myself, I took it all and revelled in their adulation. Before I knew it, I was discussing everything else I'd identified as being wrong with and in their organisation, beyond what I'd fixed myself in the short time I had available. Speaking with such clinical clarity and precision, soon I was asked to present my findings in a more appropriate setting. They wanted to use a larger conference room, this time on the top floor.

Chapter - 3.

At another time I would surely have deferred my involvement to someone else. My boss would argue that this was necessary on account of my inherent ineptitude, but the man in the mirror didn't need the support or concurrence of anyone, my boss in particular. I caught a glimpse of him again in the elevator to the executive level, barely large enough for the gathering entourage. He, I actually looked better than I had before. My clothes had not improved but my outlook as visible in my eyes was indescribable. Had I been a professional athlete I would have been seen as being in 'the zone'; focussed on a purpose and oblivious to anything beyond the playing field.

With original masterpieces on the walls and a seamless sheet of floor to ceiling glass behind a massive mahogany table, this was an appropriate setting for me to present to the cream of the company and a full house at that. No sooner had the big boss arrived that I launched into my straight off the cuff presentation. I didn't ease into my spiel with pleasantries or niceties or even small-talk, I just started. Within the first ten minutes I was stopped for no other reason than their want to bolster their audience with a greater number of translators and to enable their audio-visual team to start recording. They apologised profusely for the delay and did their best to offer distractions of food and drinks. They explained that many of their tiers of management were not as capable with the English language as they would have liked. More correctly, it was the CEO himself who did the apologising in perfect, Oxford University educated English, much to the head bowed shame of many of his staff.

When at last I was given the nod to continue, I started with a recap on what little I had already covered. My throat lubricated with a neat single malt Scotch and my blood sugar level elevated with smoked salmon and fine cheeses, I was on fire. I spoke completely devoid of humility as if oblivious to any cultural expectations that I should moderate my opinions. At first the translators faltered a little, a point which I initially attributed to their being unable to find the correct local language equivalent to capture my intent. It eventually became apparent that the CEO was keen to ensure that the translators did not soften any rhetorical body blows into something culturally amenable. He wanted his people to hear it the way I saw it. After speaking non-stop for about four hours, I paused and asked for another Scotch and any questions. I could easily have continued, but I figured I'd said enough.

Ordinarily I was only confident in English and my new found abilities did not magically extend my competencies into other languages. Still, it was obvious judging by the tone of the CEO's rant that I was happy to not be on the receiving end. One by one he appeared to chastise each of those seated around the table. Each would stand, take their verbal assault with what appeared to be un-measurable stoicism, bow, and then leave, leading their immediate team from the room. The look on the faces of each evictee and their underlings was such that I was unclear as to whether they were set to empty their desks and resign with perhaps a little dignity intact, or head to the roof directly and terminate their lives to match their careers. It was harsh, but in my mind necessary and I sat back and took it all in.

Soon only the CEO and I were left after his assistant brought a bottle commemoratively encased in a wooden box. He summonsed me away from the table while a wall behind him retracted to reveal an intimate corner with two rich leather armchairs. Facing the window as they were, the chairs assumed the look of a luxurious cockpit portal to the lights of the city far below.

We spent the next few hours and bottle of one hundred year malt discussing life and the universe. His English name was Emile. He didn't waste his time trying to tell me what his other name, his real name was. Call it Western arrogance or Eastern common sense, he either knew I wouldn't remember it, couldn't pronounce it or perhaps didn't care. He was right of course, possibly on all fronts. . He was old enough to be my father and had a distinctly paternal, familiar air about him; I liked him immediately and clearly he liked me. He was disturbingly honest and candid from the moment he removed the bottle from its box. He described this as being a worthy occasion of such an heirloom, presumably the Scotch, and how he'd initially written off my visit, a legacy of his predecessor, with disdain. Apparently he was singularly unimpressed with the perpetuation of a 'consultant knows all' mentality in favour of growing his own people, but my performance had opened his eyes. He finally appreciated the virtue which comes from someone like myself being abstracted from their company and the vested interest in preserving their own jobs. After the first glasses, I dropped all pretences of humility, not that there were many to begin with.

The receipt of a picture message from Faye, Fanny, surprised me. I hadn't so much forgotten about Faye as simply not thought about her. I'd been like a hummingbird since arriving on-site and hadn't allowed myself any time to dwell on anything beyond the task at hand. Relaxing to think about Faye, my body allowed itself to take stock of everything else that had been ignored and I hinted, less than subtly, that I needed more food.

On my return from visiting the bathroom Emile was very congratulatory. He'd unashamedly viewed a follow-up message from Faye, this time with a picture of a breast and a suggestive message written haphazardly in lipstick underneath coaxing me to bed before her return flight. He was all the more impressed when I told him that the message and Faye in general needn't have any impact on whatever plans he had in mind. I didn't mean to appear as the consummate professional, but it impressed him no end just the same. Apparently it also cemented my heterosexuality in his eyes, though I didn't realise I'd been ambiguous until this time. It seemed representative of the fact that I could do no wrong.

When Faye eventually called, Emile smiled and tolerated my half-hearted effort to delay her attempts to attract me to bed. When I ended the call, he suggested that I might prefer to partake of some local companionship instead. I knew what he meant and I didn't argue. It wasn't my style, but I'd been a corporate traveller for many years and I gathered that between the fact that I had a wedding ring and a woman waiting at the hotel he figured I wouldn't object.

But it wasn't to be. Instead, I got another call, this time from my boss. She clearly wasn't up with the latest turn of events and started to abuse me for what, in retrospect, was old news, starting with my initial lateness. When Emile heard her rant, which wasn't hard, he ushered for me to hand over the handset. I did so without question, particularly as her tirade was nothing I hadn't heard before.

Emile didn't start talking immediately. He listened quietly to the diatribe and didn't let on that she, my boss, wasn't even talking to me. After a time he rested the phone on his leg so as to speak to me. "Do you trust me?" he asked.

The old me, the usual me, would have tried to find a polite way to say 'no', but I was a new and improved model who recognised that I had no fear. Had Emile not taken the phone I could just as easily have begun some retaliatory abuse, as if there was nothing she could do to me. My heart pumped pure confidence not adrenaline, and I felt, knew I was above worry.

I told him, 'yes'. I didn't expect him to tell her I'd resigned.

He handed me the phone and I was underwhelmed with my boss's reaction. She didn't ask to confirm that she'd heard correctly, in fact I gathered she was appreciative. For all I knew, my decision had saved her from needing to make a big call, then I thought about it and realised it mightn't have even been a big call. My calendar on return from this trip had been oddly free and it was suddenly very obvious that this was perhaps my last task and I had a nasty surprise awaiting me. In retrospect, it was obvious; everyone else who'd returned from this particular client had disappeared into obscurity or later resigned. It wasn't so much a test as a plank to walk, and like a lamb to the slaughter I'd accepted the task oblivious.

My resignation was largely an anti-climax. It wasn't as if I felt relief, euphoria or anxiety. Emile made a call and soon one of his people appeared with an exquisitely chilled bottle of some Australian sparkling. He spoke authoritatively to his staff who bowed periodically in deference to whatever Emile was saying, but he did also raise his eyebrows on occasion. He left on what was surely another errand.

"Now what?" I asked Emile. He barely smiled and said nothing but poured me a glass of the wine. He told me to relax after he savoured a mouthful himself. We both sat quietly, me waiting, and Emile obviously knowing something but unwilling to share.

The door opened some time later when the assistant appeared, this time with a female accomplice. She didn't look like a colleague and for a time I struggled to assess where she fitted into the necessary corporate hierarchy. She was elegantly dressed in a Chanel business suit, but there remained considerable ambiguity as to her role and much less her purpose for being there. Not that there was any doubt, but her reaction to some instructions from Emile confirmed she was clearly substantially lower on the corporate pole.

As Emile reached for his phone, the woman began some cordial introductions, but she stopped me from standing to appear gentlemanly. Emile repeated his instruction that I relax as he nonchalantly began keying a number while this woman, I can't recall her name, leaned over me to engage the seat recline lever.

Emile saw the short-lived alarm in my eyes. It wasn't concern, just bewilderment, until this woman reached for my fly. "Relax", he said once more as he put his phone to his ear.

I started listening in to Emile's conversation but the felatio had a way of focussing my attention elsewhere. I gathered that he was talking to someone from my company, and given the jovial familiarity with which he was talking, I assumed that the person on the other end of the call was probably of the same level of management as himself. He spoke earnestly, periodically glancing my way to smile at me and perhaps to chart the woman's bobbing head. As I approached climax, I lost my ability to concentrate to any degree on what he was saying. It wasn't intentional, but we all finished together. Emile ended the call and the woman rinsed her mouth with some of my wine before standing, bowing to Emile and then she left the room, closing the door behind herself.

"Can I ask what the call was all about?" I asked, zipping myself up, still a little post orgasmic and groggy.

"Your company undervalues you and your potential contribution. I'm just helping them find the correct value," he replied as he refilled my glass.

"Isn't that irrelevant? Or are you suggesting that I should retract my resignation?"

"Far from it. I just confirmed it and told them you wouldn't lower yourself to speak with your immediate superiors on the matter."

"And that helps me how?"

"You don't need help."

For a split second I felt the familiar twangs of concern of the old me. The new me, however, understood exactly what Emile meant. My boundless capabilities were being wasted in my current, now old, position. It was so much more than just that I was a fish who had outgrown his pond. The company was bridling me, holding me back and stifling me with a corporate culture that was at odds with my potential. With my fear gone, quashed under an ocean of self-confidence, I no longer saw the job or the company in any positive light.

I thanked Emile without fervour, ambiguously between incalculable gratitude and mere acceptance. As if I was thankful for the push but downplayed his role.

Then he offered me a job and the offer was worthy of merit. As good as twice the money, options, benefits. The old me would have been apprehensive immediately, looking for a catch at first and then deciding on how to break it to my wife; sell the upside before the kicker, or to position the downside before mention of the money. The new me, however, knew that the guy wouldn't start with his best or last offer. He'd allow some room to improve, perhaps even considerable scope for improvement. He had his eyes on a winner and wasn't going to let me get away too easily. I liked his style. His getting me to resign and then removal of any means for recourse was all part of a plan. He saw an opportunity and he took it, and I decided to do the same.

I declined the offer. It had taken me a sum total of two seconds to consider then reject it, but I figured this still represented a point blank refusal. I had no second thoughts, no obsessing that maybe I ought to have considered my wife, my family, my mortgage. Emile was playing with me. "Get serious and I'll consider it," I told him. He indicated he would.

We shared a story or two until the bottle was empty before he shook my hand and sent me on my way. "Sleep on it", he said. He arranged for a car to take me back to my hotel. I accepted the ride, but not the company of the women in the back seat. As if I would be that easily placated.

Chapter - 4.

I was woken the next morning by a call from home. The kids were sick or naughty or something and I stopped listening after the first few minutes, drifting off into thought of Emile's offer. That I had options was a great way to start the day and it distracted my wife to the point of annoyance. I don't even remember how the call ended, whether it was mutual or one of us hung up on the other. Importantly, I didn't spend any time worrying about it either.

Outside, a glorious day awaited me, I could feel it. The sun shone brightly without a cloud in the sky and even as high above the sea of concrete as I was, I felt the promise of my life before me. I was tempted to commit to a walk in a park just to experience nature in its splendour. The colours were sure to be more vivid, the smells sharp and definitive, the birds distinctive and choral. Clearly my outlook had not changed overnight, though the magnitude of what I thought of myself had improved significantly. The old me was gone, not temporarily forgotten or out-voted but completely absent. My heart didn't just beat, it pulsed energy and my mind was awash with ideas and solutions. I was a new man.

I'd slept quietly. I didn't dream of anything enlightening, only simple dreams that told me that my confidence was more than just conscious. I'd dreamt I was an elephant with the dexterity of a surgeon and the foresight of an owl. That I'd fallen asleep in front of the discovery channel might possibly have had something to do with it.

Sooner or later I expected a call from my company. It was not unusual for my boss to precede my daily alarm with a call to guarantee I started the day with menaced anxiety, but I guessed she figured that I would complete my scheduled task, professionally despite my resignation. In that sense she was right in that I had already done all that I was supposed to do, and then some. Then I thought to consider that perhaps she was leaving me alone while she started some administrative ball rolling or to spread rumour and innuendo about the reasoning and circumstance of my departure. My expectations were not high and I still hadn't ruled out her being en-route to visit.

Then my phone rang again but this time caller-ID didn't hint at who the caller was, not that I needed to screen my calls. At first I thought I was being called by a telemarketer when I heard the momentary delay and secondary ringing tone and almost hung up in anticipation but I held on. Soon a mature, articulate, male voice spoke without niceties at least until after he'd confirmed who he was speaking to. Then his tone and approach changed, becoming more personal and intimate but without flippant niceties, just keeping pleasantly and politely focussed. He spoke of his discussion with Emile and only then did I figure out who he was, someone from the upper echelons of my company's hierarchy. I knew the guy's name, but not exactly whether he was at the very top of the tree or an adjacent but marginally lesser branch. To me, it didn't matter that I didn't know *exactly* who he was as I didn't need to pay him any undue respect or deference. I didn't need anything from him.

The guy made some effort to share his greater vision of a powerful company. He spoke of big numbers and growth and an immediate and ongoing need for good people. Not surprisingly, he then went on to explain that I was amongst the people that he'd been searching for, and how overwhelmed he'd been to have this fact brought to his attention by an outsider. As he continued, I considered going on the attack for his corporate ethos and particular managers who had kept such good people hidden from view, but I held my tongue. Eventually he got to the action end of his call and asked if I was serious and committed in my resignation or whether he could write it off as a well-intentioned and impeccably timed effort to leverage a better compensation package.

I told him it was no ruse and that I'd consider anything that he was prepared to offer, just as I was considering what Emile had put forward. He fished for the figure, the package that might have me 'stay' to which I replied that any counter offer would need to be exceptional to make me 'join'.

The call didn't so much meet its natural conclusion as fizzle out. Presumably he got the impression that I was not going to be persuaded or convinced over the phone. I vaguely recall him suggesting that an in person meeting would be better.

Chapter - 5.

Every adult knows that time is a precious commodity. There's only 24 hours each day and it's never enough. Perhaps if you were only interested in work *or* a life it might be possible to achieve everything that's necessary in *your* life between sunrises. My boss only seemed to be interested in work and she seemed to manage, perhaps because her pursuit also gave her the delight of watching me struggle. She probably never slept judging by the continual stream of emails she managed to send all day and night, so that certainly would have made available more time for evil. Maybe in sucking the life out of me, and others, she'd found a way to cheat the clock.

However, a work-life balance always eluded me. Between work, home and rest I was continually behind in at least one if not all aspects. No matter how or what I'd tried, I never managed to get it right. I'd done no end of time management training, read countless books on the subject and while I was technically an expert, there was no mistaking the fact that it didn't help. I knew what to do, classifying every epoch, every single minute of the day for purpose and importance. I'd trimmed the fat out of my life and tuned my timetable to the limits of both doctrine and practicality, but it hadn't worked. On top of everything else, I never really got a moment for myself and certainly never got time to think. Here I was though, alone in a hotel room with nothing to do but think and not a stress to distract me. My mind left to roam I could have solved the world's problems probably, but first I needed to make sense of what was happening and why.

I'd never been a particularly good student or academic, but I recognised and appreciated true genius. Science was never really my 'thing' but I loved the theories about energy being in a state of equilibrium. That all matter in the universe is ultimately constant only changing form was amazing in its simplicity. I marvelled at how this theory was adapted in economic and financial circles to explain bull and bear markets, and also the universal distribution of wealth. I guess I could account for the tides in this same way; the amount of water in the oceans remained the same, it just moved around.

Not religious by any means, I attributed everything in my life to the same universe. I was a simple man at heart treating time with my family with all its foibles as good, and time away as the inevitable *yin* for my *yang*. Over the course of my life I figured that I would break even, achieve the nirvana of equilibrium. Through this mindset I took the bad bits knowing, expecting or hoping that something good would come. If I wasn't travelling, if I'd ever paused to think about it, I would expect my boss to tell me another trip was necessary. If she ever sensed I was making headway or enjoying life at the time, the trip would require an immediate departure and be of an uncertain duration, but not to expect to be released inside a month; long enough to register a definitive void in my home life, not just a blip. Perhaps if I was looking forward to some event, a birthday or weekend away, she'd gloat that the trip might just jeopardise that. Thus my life was the sum of good and bad, my family on one side and my boss on the other. But now my boss was not in the picture. I felt like a drowning man suddenly without the dunking foot of inevitability to continually push me under. Not only could I now stay afloat, but I could swim to rescue myself.

Full of myself as I was though, I still recognised that my life was sure to still be the balance of good and bad and while typically I never planned for a reversal of fortune when things were going well, now I realised that change was inevitable. I also understood that any turn in my fortune would need to be of a higher order too, unless I was to disprove the theory upon which the universe was dependent. That realisation helped me no end. By extension, I knew that how I felt wasn't going to last forever. As capable as I felt, it was too much to even imagine that the new me would stick around indefinitely. As great as that might be, the odds against it were just too high.

Knowing this, I well understood that I had two basic options open to me. I could retreat and consolidate my gains in anticipation of everything turning sour, or I could ride my success for as long as it lasted. I could have spent an inordinate amount of time deliberating my choice until it occurred to me that both required me to get dressed.

I took my time in the shower, particularly as it was my first for a few days. It didn't invigorate me, it really just made me clean, just as shaving didn't prepare me for the day. I was primed and ready for anything that the world could throw at me.

After cutting my finger on a shard of glass I realised that my aftershave bottle had smashed in my bag. It annoyed me a little but in essence this only proved that my new found positivity had not pushed me into some fairy-tale break from reality. I could have tolerated the prospect of smelling like a department store perfumery but I wasn't prepared to wear a shirt pierced across the breast pocket; to do so would have undermined how I felt.

The concierge then hand delivered word that Emile's car would be waiting at the very reasonable time of 10am. Without any pressing need to force my hand and wear my aromatic clothes for fear of being late to work, I figured this gave me the opportunity for an impromptu shopping trip.

I re-dressed in my dirty clothes and left the hotel and cast my eyes left and right. On one side were the shops that obviously were intended to appeal to my budget and to the other were the better shops, appealing to the better healed. Had my wife been with me she would have wanted to go one way but ended up going the other; I would have gone back inside foregoing the shopping altogether.

I decided at that moment that I'd look as I felt. I headed for what my wife would have described as 'decent' stores, but what I would have considered just expensive.   As I sauntered past the likes of Vuitton and Boss, I had flashbacks of me doing the same thing at home a year ago; walking fast, eyes forward, not bothering to consider the possibilities. This time however I got a vibe from one particular store and waited at the door until I was noticed by the staff but ultimately ignored. The ordinary me would have taken their reluctance to serve me in my dishevelled state with reasonable grace. The few prices visible were offensively high and in the entire shop I didn't see any signage featuring the word 'sale'. My time waiting to be noticed, however, gave me a chance to look around without interruption.

Haute couture is timeless. I was reminded of this as I looked at what was on offer. One of my gay friends would have pointed out the subtleties of cut, fabric and length, but all I saw were similar suits, any of which would probably have worked for me. Pending any staff interest, I proved my commitment and crossed the threshold towards the racks. I felt like a philistine as I marvelled at the apparent differences between 'Tibetan Midnight' and 'Eclipse'; particularly as I would have called them each 'black'. I laughed openly, and this finally earned me some attention.

Had my wife been present, she would have described what 'I' wanted, leaving me to just detail my size. Being on my own, I expected to flounder somewhat when confronted by the woman, but I didn't. I offered a farcical explanation for my less than perfect appearance then deposited my corporate card on the counter and told her to tend to me. That the card would be subject to governance and scrutiny was not my concern. Technically I wasn't even an employee which would make any purchase all the more sweet.

She assured me that I could expect focussed and hands-on attention and produced a tape measure as a token of commencement. She measured me all over and I finally felt tended to. When finished, she made a puzzled expression and explained that I was an unusual shape: tall but not large, trim not slim and fit without being chunky. I couldn't have cared less, except for the fact that it meant they apparently had a whole range that would fit straight off the rack. She marvelled that my measurements were so perfect that it was as if I was the manikin that must have been used for the clothing design and manufacture. At first she produced a single suit and led me to a large changing room to try it on.

I'd never experienced a really nice suit before, not like this. Now I felt substantial, like the clothes matched the man inside. My elevated mood was still further enhanced, and I loved how I looked. Then several suits of different styles were serialised for me to try and I liked each a little more than the last. Far from being indecisive, I told the woman I'd buy any that I liked and cast my old clothes into a rubbish bin as if to confirm my intent. With each new article the woman's attentiveness increased significantly and with each item I felt my self-esteem even more bolstered. I didn't limit my attention to outer wear either, choosing matching accessories, belts, business shirts, casual wear, two pairs of shoes, and even underwear that was both comfortable and made me look like I had a savage mongoose down my trousers.

As the woman's demeanour progressed to exuberance, I appreciated that I already had more than I could reasonably carry on my own in my newly selected suitcases, but also that I didn't feel like I had what I'd come for. In looking over what I'd chosen I came to the conclusion I was still being restricted. I had chosen safe styles in a variety of fabrics, albeit in a selection of vivid colours, but nothing to really make a statement. That's when I cast a reviewing eye over the display window.

My wife had been a window dresser for a time and through her I understood the purpose behind these displays, particularly in a store offering such finery. Their intent was to highlight what was possible, not really what was probable. Now however I became fixated on a suit like no other. It was intended to blur the divide between East and West, with European lines and Italian tailoring but with a Mandarin collar. Most of all I focussed on the colour. Fire engine red silk. The more I looked, the more I considered it an option and it very quickly crossed the chasm from possible to probable. "And that", I said to the woman, pointing, half expecting her to offer some dismissive explanation, but she didn't. Perhaps I underestimated the arrogance of the well shod.

She retrieved the suit and inspected the hand written size information on the tag. She told me it would fit without alteration and that it was a one of a kind. I told her it would suit me perfectly. She brought an appropriate white shirt and matching red shoes made of the softest leather I'd ever felt. Just touching them felt illicit, as if the leather came from some endangered or extinct species, or even a political prisoner.

Not able to contain my exuberance, I dressed as if in a frenzy to see myself re-invented. The suit looked excellent on display but exquisite on me, I knew it but the look on the woman's face when I exited the changing room said it all. She didn't say anything, not that I heard anyway. Perhaps she offered inanities, heartfelt or otherwise, but I didn't hear them. I finally looked as I felt and I didn't need to hear the adulation of others to prove a point. I would stand out in any crowd and my attire would give warning as to what the world was up against in me.

I don't even know what it all cost after having just signed the sales slip as it was graciously coaxed in my direction. There was no question of exceeding the open limit necessary to cover all of my travel expenses, so I didn't even bother with any mental arithmetic. What was more, I deserved it. The woman was clearly excited at the prospect of her commission and I appreciated that she didn't try to hide it with feigned pleasantries.

Leaving the trivialities of getting all of my new purchases back to my hotel to the woman, I just enjoyed the brief walk. The crowds parted before me as I cut a swathe through the masses. Buoyed as I was and resplendent in my new look, I didn't even allow my phone ringing in my pocket to interrupt my mood.

Chapter - 6.

The call was from Emile. He didn't ask if I'd considered his offer, only to perform a task for him. It was a request, nothing more. It didn't feel as if it was a test or that doing it would represent tacit acceptance of his job offer. It was just something ambiguously between favour and obligation. My task was simply to visit his competitor and do unto them what I'd done the day before with his organisation. The way he described it, I was just to appear and shine, just like the sun would in all its' predictability.

His car met me outside my hotel and raced me across town in more than adequate luxury. I had no idea where I was going, but it wasn't as if I felt I was going to be met with a situation I couldn't handle wherever I was taken.

My arrival at another towering office building was met with a crowd but no fanfare, though I could sense the expectation around me. I was led without introduction to the top floor conference room with bare civility. This boardroom was similar to Emile's. For all I knew of the city skyline, I might have been able to see Emile's very office through the glass, had I been given the opportunity.

I was seated, or rather, asked to sit at the table and told to wait. I felt the suppressive effect of a humourless formality in the office.   There was no light-hearted discussion in any language, let alone banter to include me from any of the 17 greying men seated at the table, each waiting patiently, their suit jackets still buttoned and palms splayed wide on the table. Behind each was a staff of one or two standing only marginally more relaxed, documents held close to their chest except for occasions when some device demanded their attention. They would furtively be distracted before returning to their waiting stance.

I waited 10 minutes, during which time no-one spoke to me and barely even a word was whispered amongst anyone else. Eventually, I stood and decided to inspect the décor of the room, ignoring disapproving looks and cajoling comments. The artwork all looked too pretentious for my liking, but it seemed that what was important was to demonstrate that I was prepared to challenge the regime. A purist might have assumed that much was obvious just looking at how I was dressed.

If I'd believed my suit had any magical power before this time, I had my theory confirmed. High into the smog as we were, I felt the pollution dissipate to allow a block of sunlight to further illuminate me. I pictured myself walking around the room, cursory interest in my surrounds oblivious to my suit turning technicolour like Joseph's dream-coat and changing hue with each step. I spared a thought for what everyone else assembled would have made of the spectacle.

The sunlight disappeared as the doors opened. A single man entered and someone made a comment, the purpose of which being to apparently confirm that everyone was on their feet. Heads were bowed everywhere, except mine. I could just as easily have resumed my position at the table. Nobody asked me or told me what was expected, but I wasn't so naive as to be oblivious. I just didn't feel like being that compliant.

I brushed the front of my suit as if to remove some imaginary lint in an effort to improve my appearance, but in reality I did it to draw further attention to myself. Then I marched to the man, unconcerned at the look of amazement from everyone, particularly him, stopping just shy of the guy and clicked my heels together in a fascist manner. Had I actually slapped his face I wouldn't have had any more of his attention. I lowered my eyelids simultaneously as an arrogant faux bow and presented my hand.

That he didn't immediately accept or return the handshake made me initially wonder if the guy was some Howard Hughes-like germophobe who preferred his contact via intermediaries, but I wasn't interested in any of his monkeys. I wanted to present myself to the organ-grinder himself. I stared the man down until he softened a little to accept my hand. His handshake was placid and more than a little sweaty and I knew who intimidated who.

"I see that all I have heard is true", he said in accented, but still good English, albeit in broken trigrams as if he'd learnt the language by translating a few words at a time.

"What do you need?" I asked, standing before him with my arms casually beside me, as much to keep my suit perfect as to maintain my position of power. He politely gestured for me to return to my allocated seat. I sauntered casually and took my place, happy I could still dominate proceedings from there.

The guy was of the same mindset as Emile had been. He explained in his stilted fashion that while he was reluctant to enlist the input of external consultants, they were in need of 'specialist guidance'. Not wanting to appear backward in coming forward, at this I launched into a tirade at his childish, naïve, fourteenth century mindset. I didn't set any expectation I'd help, only that I'd listen.

One by one, his people subjected me to a slideshow based presentation of their cog's particular role in the greater organisational machine. Someone would speak and one of his cronies, they were all men, would point as appropriate to relevant facts or metrics on the screen using a truncheon sized laser pointer.

I took it all in, absorbing everything I heard and saw. Here was an organisation in trouble, 1950's style management in a twenty second century niche and pre-Y2K business model. My only problem was where to begin. I felt like stopping the presentations after a few hours, but I let them continue even though I'd heard enough after the first hour. It wasn't until I received a text message from Emile that I finally said 'Uncle' and stopped the show. His message detailed projections of the savings and profit of my recommendations from the day before and this buoyed me enough to end the tedium.

I took centre-stage and started using antics that I recalled seeing from some documentary about Hitler's Nuremberg rallies. I waited until eyes were on me, took a deep breath as if I was about to speak, paused, and then stepped back from the pseudo-dais. Hitler was a good orator, but I was better. I had them salivating, edging forward in their seats in anticipation, waiting for me to begin. When eventually I did speak it was to ask for a scotch and that it had better be the good stuff.

As I savoured quite a nice malt, I wondered if my observations, what I thought, and ultimately my recommendations, would have been possible by anyone else, beit the old me or a far more capable individual than I was ordinarily. I decided that while it might have been possible by another, they couldn't 'sell' it like I could. To do so would be professional suicide. Others would pander around what needed to be said, bound by the shackles of decorum, eyes on the on-going gravy train and consultative or professional longevity. I, on the other hand, held no apprehension as to the future. I was going to live and behave in the 'now' confident that later would be another 'now'.

When I thought I'd kept them hanging for long enough I started and didn't hold back. With no eyes on any prize and no thinking of how my boss would rate or belittle my performance, I just spoke as if I'd been asked for 'my' opinion and what I'd do to address the greater systemic failure as if it were up to me.

Unrestrained, I meticulously proceeded to destroy everything that had been presented to me, not out of spite but because it was necessary; this is what I was here for. I was on fire and I made my argument into a seamless, consolidated case. I followed up my forthrightness with their own metrics, perfectly memorised and recalled, to substantiate all of my observations and subsequent recommendations. I called for the sacking of those who didn't impress me, evidenced in their brief time in the spotlight. I laid the groundwork for organisational restructures, facility closures, software architectural re-direction, and corporate vision re-alignment. My speech had taken two full hours, almost to the minute.

Jaws were agape and from this I gathered that they didn't expect to have a light shone on them with such brutality. Whether I told them anything they didn't already know was anyone's guess. I didn't waste time thinking whether any of them or any prior consultant was comparable to me, now or ever. They didn't confess anything to me after that, perhaps they were too scared of my critical analysis.

I was not without error though. After I held the senior guy personally responsible for presiding over the biggest shambles since world war one, it was unlikely he was going to offer me another drink. He was escorted from the room by security to which I only shrugged and vainly hoped that my glass would be topped up.

Someone explained that the security was just a precaution and that I shouldn't read too much into it, but like a true consultant I was beyond concern for whether my recommendations were acted upon.

I figured it was time I left. I excused myself and headed straight for Emile's office.

Chapter - 7.

"You did well", Emile began as soon as his assistant escorted me into his private office. It was stately and more like a manor library than a corporate executive's chamber. Two walls were a mass of bookcases the full width and right up to the fifteen foot ceilings. How anyone would reach the books on the top shelves without any visible ladder interested me. Maybe it didn't come up often, or more likely he just said what he wanted and thereafter it became someone else's problem. To me it represented practical power and it appealed.

"Your suit is very becoming," Emile began. "Excuse the pun, but it 'suits' you."

I smiled and overlooked the cliché, knowing exactly what he meant. "Why did you want me to visit that company today?" I asked with passing interest as I slumped myself into one of his luxurious leather arm-chairs. "They were a joke."

He poured me a drink after checking his watch. "A joke they may be but you were the first to have cut through their spin and told them what was necessary."

"So why did you point me at them?"

"Perhaps I wanted to see how you'd perform entirely on your own," said Emile. "On that score you did well and word travels fast from such engagements."

I shrugged. "So what now?"

Emile stood looking out his window, hands behind his back. "I'd suggest you are to be courted."

"By who? Whom?" I asked, gargling some of the scotch as a subtle suggestion that it was not of the calibre of the previous evening.

"Me. The crowd you insulted today, your *old* employer."

"I don't think it's fair to say I insulted them," I challenged with conviction, glossing over the intent of Emile's comment. "I don't think I said anything that didn't *need* to be said. With the possible exception of the head honcho, I kept it reasonably professional and devoid of personalities. He pissed me off so I went the extra mile."

"Accepted."

"So? What's the problem?"

"For me or you?" Emile teased. He continued after he saw an inkling of annoyance on my face. "That I put you into their organisation will be overlooked in the interests of a greater benefit. Your recommendations stand to make and save them millions. However, 'face' is most important in this part of the world and he's just lost a lot of face."

"So?"

"The problem is that you just professionally castrated him and he's decidedly well connected."

"So? You put me into the situation and you never told me about his connections."

"True, but you probably wouldn't have moderated your assault for any reason even if you'd known. Right?"

Emile had a point. "So what's going to happen now?" I asked.

"How long until you leave the country?"

"I don't suppose he'd accept his culpability as some mitigation."

"Quite," Emile said. "Just be aware he has powerful and dangerous allies. For that point, don't forget everyone with power has enemies."

I skulled the last of my drink and waited for the refill, arrogantly shrugging off Emile's comment but I recognised the point he was making. For the first time in several days I felt mortal and that I had something to fear. I thought it would constrain my mood, at least marginally, but it didn't. I'd long appreciated the jolt that a little fear could have on my higher functioning, and it had proven itself useful. The stress my boss imposed on me had become a tool I'd used to focus and squeeze a little extra from my throughput. This, however, was different.

I knew it wasn't adrenaline; my body wasn't preparing for any 'fight or flight'. Rather, it was as if my attitude, my innate invincibility, was being further tuned. It was like my soul appreciated the reminder that I was still biologically a fragile mass of proteins and cells encased in skin. That I was so much above those around me while still biologically similar made me even more mindful of my capacity. "I bet I'll earn some notoriety from my efforts. I sense my blue book value going up accordingly."

"Quite true," Emile confessed. "Your ex-boss and I discussed that very point today in person while you were otherwise engaged."

I held back my surprise. That she would have come was not entirely unexpected and I'd initially anticipated as much. That she'd not shown her face was also well within her character and for a time I wondered what she was up to. I didn't stress about it though; that's what the old me would have done. Instead, I likened her actions to those of a chess opponent and I strategised as to a counter move. "What did she want?"

Emile let slip a coy smile and this interested me. "She tried to distance herself from you."

"So did you put her right?"

"No," said Emile with a grin. "Though, I did later talk to her higher, reprimanding her for her fickle managerial style."

"Thanks, but I can fight my own battles." I appreciated Emile's intentions, but it felt appropriate to reiterate my self-assurance. "I'm actually more appreciative for what I can only imagine would have been the look on her face."

"True. No sooner had I gotten off the phone that her phone started to ring. That I made her continue to felate me while she received her reprimand surely would have helped consolidate the magnitude of her error."

I felt an odd and unexpected emotion. The more I thought about it and pictured Emile's satisfaction with this puppet-master servicing him, the more I wanted. Fixated with unrequited anger, it was as if my long-corralled loathing was being released. I liked this even more than I liked the newfound but now familiar feel of justified self-confidence.

I had long since known the lure of heroin to the addict. After an ankle reconstruction some years ago, I understood the body's desire for opiates and how the mind would crave increasingly more product. I felt the same desire and craving now, as if revenge was a drug and I wondered how I might improve the sensation. The most obvious means was to repeat the hit. I could beat her while she was down, draw attention to her misdirected efforts. For all I knew, I was on the cusp of substantial local and possibly international publicity and I could use this time in the spotlight to emphasise her malfeasance, overtly or covertly. This strategy had merit which I understood immediately. I foresaw myself revelling at her misery and toasting the potential for her marginalisation, but I also saw the hit as being short-lived. More importantly, that I would not have a particularly active role in her demise would play on me, I could feel it. It was active involvement that was going to make the difference between short-lived high and on-going recollective ecstasy. At that very moment I knew I wanted to really participate in her downfall.

Emile drew me back into the present after my daydreaming. "You know she'd probably try to make amends if you wanted. I found her to be very receptive to the suggestion, and she didn't need too much encouragement."

"You're assuming I want her to make amends."

"Moving on is important. It is the mark of true greatness in many religions and cultures," Emile said philosophically.

"You don't have the same vested interest in this as I do. So it's easy for you to be noble." I wasn't trying to provoke Emile, but it was a fair point which deserved explanation. For years she'd been the embodiment of the burden of my life. The incessant abuse and belittlement, the countless trips and the perpetual fatigue all had a human face and I was unwilling to wipe the slate clean. For years, amid all of my resentment I'd wanted to say something or retaliate. God knows I'd even considered assaulting her, punching the bitch in the face each time I was derided to tear-point or my life was impacted by work travel. Each time I'd show restraint, internalise my anger into stress and compartmentalise it away like a time-bomb sure to manifest itself as cancer the day I retired. In the past, I would try to appease myself that in so doing I was proving my inner strength, that such retaliation would hurt me more. My sacking, professional blacklisting and surely a criminal record would give *her* the last laugh. But that was the old me.

The new me had a different perspective entirely. Inspired by my new capabilities I re-appraised my boss's actions, trying to understand what had happened. Cornered, in trouble and in the spotlight, I saw how Emile's suggestion would have appealed. She had nothing to lose and maybe Emile had offered professional absolution for a few minute's 'work'. Maybe Emile didn't offer anything in return. Maybe my boss didn't do it out of fear. I'd resisted the temptation to associate my boss's near meteoric rise to power with sexual favours because it was just too clichéd to be realistic, but now I wasn't sure. Maybe she did. Maybe she didn't. Distracted with my line of thought as I was, I didn't hear Emile's comment until he repeated himself.

"I said you should be careful. I can see your capabilities as clearly as I can see through this glass. And in much the same way you need to be mindful that, like glass, you are not indestructible." He made a fist and knocked heavily on the window. "Even bullet-proof glass, which this isn't incidentally, can be breached and on several occasions little birds have sacrificed themselves to prove that very point."

Full of myself as I was, I wasn't really listening. It must have been obvious to Emile who saw fit to continue. "I'm not saying that your success is as fickle as this glass, only that your capabilities will have limitations."

I disagreed.

Chapter - 8.

There was a comfort between Emile and I. He didn't feel any compulsion to say anything that didn't need to be said, and likewise I didn't feel obligated to talk unless I had something worthy of sharing. Had I asked where we were going, had I really cared, I'm sure he would have explained, but I'd been wined and dined enough over the years to know the deal and be realistic in my expectations. I just sat in the back seat and watched the world outside the limousine.

Emile received a phone call while we were in the car heading for what I hoped would be dinner. I gathered it was from his wife before he switched to speaking in English, as if doing so would confirm that there were no secrets between us. I'd heard his type of conversation before. I'd had this type of conversation before myself.

His wife was lonely and just wanted to talk. Ideally she wanted him home earlier than midnight for the first time in a long while, but it was clear she'd settle in the meantime for a simple few words. I gathered this was part of their routine; she'd telephone perhaps at this same time every day, they'd share a few banalities and life would go on, perhaps until he'd join her in bed, share a few hours asleep before waking to do it all again. It made me miss my wife.

Emile didn't make any effort to end the call, but he was hardly an active participant in the conversation either. He took the inevitability of the talk in good grace, but there was no emotion that would have been received through his words or the manner that they were said. The moment the call ended he continued with our prior conversation as if he'd spent his time only passively communicating with his wife but in reality he was actively planning our time together.

Our dinner venue suggested fine dining and floor length pristine white linen tablecloths raised my expectations. I was more than a little disappointed to have to part with my suit jacket at the door; I felt so good in it that I was reluctant to shed it. I felt the same for my need to remove my shoes; my lovely shoes that only after they were off did I really appreciate just how comfortable they were and started to miss them.

Clearly Emile was a regular, known by various staff judging by the non-cursory smiles, and by patrons on adjoining tables evidenced in their cocktail gestures. I didn't get the same impression from the women waiting for us at what was most certainly Emile's usual table. These were professionals and unashamedly so. I don't know whether I expected anything different. Emile was out to impress me obviously, but I couldn't rightly gauge if this was to be achieved with any real effort on his part. Was tonight's dinner with extras to be an exhibition purely for my benefit, or was it just another night? Then again, I didn't really care.

I treated the women for the decorations that they were. They were beautiful, polite and pleasant enough, but I ignored them just the same. I let them make their small-talk, I laughed at their jokes and complimented them on their obvious effort to sound knowledgeable and more than just expensive prostitutes. Of course, they described themselves as models and that they were where they were, here right now, on business. I immediately saw their joke; Emile and I were business. I wasn't rude to them, I just preferred to speak to Emile.

I doubted that Emile was as open to other outsiders typically as he was with me. I sensed genuine warmth and I hoped my arrogance allowed something to be returned to him. We spoke about everything and nothing in particular. If anything, we glossed over the typical shallow topics that usually dominated professional but casual discussion. We didn't search for any sport or humorous anecdote that might span our cultural and continental divides. Instead, we focussed on more human, deeper topics, as if we had real history in our friendship.

Eventually, Emile made mention of his son. It wasn't as if he'd made any conscious effort to avoid or steer our conversation that way, only that his son was an inevitable point of discussion. He proudly showed me photos from his wallet, laminated as if to protect them from repeated examination. Only then did I begin to understand why Emile had warmed to me. He'd raised his son to follow in his footsteps, but somewhere along the way it became obvious that business was not in his breeding. If he didn't look so much like Emile, apparently there could have been serious question as to his paternity, but it never got to that. The guy killed himself in some opiate and alcohol fuelled binge that was attributed solely to stress. Emile took all of the credit, or blame, for the stress that took its toll on his son stoically. It was as if he'd accepted his role so often that now he was just sharing his guilt with another party.

I can't even remember what I ate for my meal. I know that it must have been good as my memory seems to work better with things that I'd rather forget. It was probably steak as I seem to prefer the most expensive thing on the menu when I'm not paying. I do recall that our female escorts ate salad which at the time spoke volumes as to provide some authenticity to their claim to be models. It didn't make them more interesting though, and I continued my frank discussion with Emile right until I felt the need to freshen up.

When I returned to the table, the women were conspicuous in their absence. I'd done little more than tolerate them and I looked forward to being able to continue our more candid conversation without the distractions. I gathered that Emile had asked them to go while I was elsewhere. He had a look on his face that suggested acceptance that his evening was not going to go entirely to plan. Secretly, I wondered if his wife was going to be appreciative for my part in putting a dampener in his plans.

Emile was distracted, considerably more than I figured he would be after all that he'd disclosed. It seemed appropriate that I end the evening there and then and decided to leave him alone with his thoughts and walk back to my hotel.

Chapter - 9.

The highs and lows of the first few days of travel eventually settle into a mundane work rhythm which I knew well. Work, go back to my little box with its bed and TV, eventually sleep and wake the following morning ready to do it all again. My boss's expectation is that I spend every waking hour working, exploiting the lack of distractions, effectively doubling my throughput as I continue with my usual job after hours while my daylight hours are focussed on the task that necessitated my travel. A long time ago I'd been tempted, naïvely thinking I might make headway or even get in front with my workload when there's nothing else to do away from the 'distractions of home'. I thought my boss might interpret my actions as dedication and it might earn me some credit, but it was a ploy and afterwards she made it clear that my efforts were now what she expected all the time. After that stunt my norm became long hours in the office and more hours from home with only the minimum of sleep to allow me to continue indefinitely.

As I walked back to my hotel I thought of what I could do to break the monotony of my standard working day. I hadn't checked the offerings of my hotel, but it was likely that it featured some alternatives, possibly something healthy, invariably at least a room with a static gym and an exercise bike. They would call it something impressive, like 'Health Club' and sometimes the name alone was enough to tempt me to visit at least once. In the past I'd imagined my wife's reaction when I came home hard-bodied, buff and physically invigorated after taking time out during a trip, but somewhere along the way it lost its' appeal. Perhaps it's just me, but the idea of sweating it out in an undersized, poorly ventilated room filled with less equipment than my own garage doesn't really sound worth it. Even so, I knew I had clothes waiting in my old suitcase like I always did, just in case I found the motivation and some sinus infection allowed me to withstand the smell of other travellers' sweat.

I walked past bars and restaurants filled with lonely men, invariably travellers like me, some with the foresight to have brought a book with them to read so as to feel less conspicuous, at least until the alcohol sets in. When first I started to travel I used to smirk at anyone eating, fork in one hand and fat paperback in the other, but once you've experienced how exposed you feel without the crutch of a distraction or company, you understand. They sat or stood with sullen pre-drunken bored eyes considering their options and probably stressing at the pointlessness of their lives. This time at least, I would not join them.

As I drew nearer to my hotel, companionship was for sale on every street corner. I'm sure it was my boss's little joke that most of the hotels her people stayed in while travelling were invariably situated in the middle of unofficial red-light districts. By day they might pass a seediness test, but by night the preponderance of company for hire left no mistake. I was tempted by a seemingly endless array of women in varying states of undress as I walked to the hotel. They'd approach me in my power-suit, brazenly figuring that I was liable to ask for anything and everything and all they had to do was negotiate a price, but I just walked past, much to their surprise. I did, however, consider the potential for an endless stream of flesh and fluids and wondered how many I could service before I lost interest, sensation or adequate blood pressure. The important thing is that I didn't, I could have, but I didn't. I was more powerful than I'd imagined.

Chapter - 10.

When I returned to my hotel, alone, the duty manager stopped me in the elevator. He handed me an envelope and a phone as if he'd been briefed to co-ordinate the call and the intercept as soon as I entered the lobby. I noted the measured look of relief on his face, satisfied that he'd completed an important task.

The call was from my CEO again. I listened while reading a fax from the envelope, but after a time I gathered that he was simply reinforcing or repeating the letter, effectively an invitation to head office; first class of course. He obviously expected me to be non-committal and he started insisting, emphasising that I had 'nothing to lose'. I thought he should have suggested that I had 'everything to gain' and I told him so.

I'd never been to head office. Sure, I'd been to New York, but never to the corporate headquarters as I'd never been good enough or had any real occasion to go. I'd imagined the stifling, formal air and it was not something I aspired to and for years my take had been reciprocated; they didn't want me either. But now I had something they wanted. More correctly, I was what they wanted.

The timing of the flight didn't sit well with me. It would have meant a rush to pack up my room and then a race across town to the airport. To be fair, I never unpacked my suitcase, let alone my new cases which I assumed would be in my room, so re-packing would not take that long, but I was in no mood to experience any time related stress. The hotel manager conceded that my room had already been vacated in anticipation and the hotel car was waiting.

He said it with such shame that I patted him on the shoulder, as if I well understood that it was not his decision to make.

I agreed to the impromptu visit, not reluctantly but as if I had nothing else pressing and felt like the flight. I allowed myself to be escorted to the car and enjoyed the solid thud of quality engineering as the door of the Mercedes closed behind me and discovered that Emile was waiting in the back seat. I started to marvel as to how he could have beat me to my hotel but he cut me short and upped his offer while handing me a filled glass of sparkling.

I really appreciated the way that Emile didn't mix platitudes with a big sell, banter with shop-talk. He didn't labour any point, he just told me that he and I could work closely together beautifully and that the foundations of truly great business empires are laid on such relationships. As expected, his package offer had improved substantially, so much so that I focussed less on the money than on the possibilities of the role and the power that I could wield.

He also didn't demand that I make any decision right there and then, in spite of his obvious confidence that I would come to join him, eventually. He was intelligent enough to appreciate that I would consider other offers and that I wouldn't reduce myself to accept the first offer. He dropped me at the international terminal and shook my hand amicably as if to reinforce his offer while emphasising something special in our new relationship.

Chapter - 11.

First class was full of faces, only a few of which I recognised from movies or various tabloids. If ever there was a time when I would have expected some 'extra attention', this flight was it, but as it was my attendant was keen to service only my every non-sexual whim, not that I lowered myself to ask.

Like Pavlov's dog, I normally associated the chimes when we were airborne with food, but also professional stresses. That I'm offered a biscuit when once I would have received an actual meal is the result of one of my kind. The corporate bean counters get the blame, but the reality is that some managerial consultant like me would have put forward the value proposition, emphasising the waste and the potential for savings. The economic rationalists would have agreed and the consultant would have been paid handsomely for their role in corporate improvement. Oppenheimer apparently always felt guilt for his creation and while my 'achievements' were far less grandiose, I still felt on-going stress. I wonder if Oppenheimer would have felt more or less guilt had his mentor or superiors invested so much time or effort in indoctrinating him as my boss had done. Brainwashed by my boss, I use words like 'streamlining process' and 'business efficiency' to explain how my client organisation might improve their bottom line. The sterility of my choice of words is deliberate, hiding the fact that these 'savings' all typically involve shedding heads, reducing the numbers of employees or removing services which ultimately result in job losses elsewhere. I try not to look at it that way, but each cabin chime forces a wave of anxiety through me just the same, as if the sub-conscious good in me was rising up against my professionally programmed evil conscious.

Oddly, those stresses were absent on this flight. This time when I heard the chime I only loosened my seatbelt and settled myself in for what I knew would be excellent cuisine. I almost felt sorry for everyone back in economy class knowing that *their* meal service would be nothing special. In much the same way I partook of the slippers and designer pyjamas offered to me knowing full well that the masses would be lucky to get a disposable washcloth. I thought about the consultant who identified the 'waste' of giveaways, cheap plastic combs and under-appreciated food, whoever he or she was. I wondered for a time if that particular consultant lost any sleep or felt any regret for their actions just as I'd done almost continually.

I had a vacant seat beside me and after the meal service was complete, I enjoyed the attendant in her lesser known role of travellers' companion. She and I sat and talked for much of the flight. I can't really recall what we spoke about. It certainly wasn't particularly memorable for any reason other than that we were talking. There was nothing sexual or flirtatious and in fact I actually enjoyed that our conversation was not laced in innuendo.

Only in retrospect did I appreciate that the appeal of our talk was the acceptance that I was missing the companionship of my wife. I missed the way that my wife and I communicated, what was said and what wasn't, possibly because it didn't need to be said. That getting her a coffee or breakfast in bed at home, whenever I was home, spoke more than idle banter meant a lot to me. But here I was, talking for hours with an indentured stranger as we slid across the Pacific. I felt guilty. I hadn't spoken to my wife for days and here I was talking to the flight attendant. I hadn't shared news of my remarkable transformation, my resignation or even the accumulating offers with my family, and yet maybe I'd mentioned it to this stranger. Maybe I told her my story or even enlisted her advice, I can't recall. I hoped that in whatever we spoke about I'd spoken adequately highly of my own family.

Chapter - 12.

The flight attendant was called from my side not long after we crossed the international dateline. If nothing else, this gave me a chance to get some sleep. While I didn't feel fatigued, I knew I was surely not above the effects of jetlag. My usual solution to jetlag is always to live in the destination time-zone, no matter how hard. So if I arrive in the morning after a red-eye, the first day is long and hard, but thereafter it improves. My strategy doesn't work if I'm continually changing time-zones though. On that front, my experience tells me that nothing helps other than to try to rest each day as best I can.

Distant in the lap of luxury, I almost didn't notice when my flight was redirected to Denver. The pilot described the fault as generally as he was obligated. Whether this meant he half expected the wings to drop off or that there'd been a bomb scare, I didn't rightly know and didn't ask. Similarly, I didn't care if the rabble back in coach were in a pre-death frenzy. I just sat back and asked for another sparkling to tide me over.

When we landed, the airline ensured that those from first class were quickly through immigration and informed as to the airlines' efforts to arrange the continuation of their journey. I gathered from the obvious anger of most passengers that this decency did not extend to economy class judging by the prevailing animosity to any staff member in uniform. Apparently I'd have to wait for six hours, which seemed an inordinately long time, but I didn't mind. The unscheduled stop off was no real inconvenience to me. That I was here or in New York was no great matter when my life was elsewhere still.

When I was in familiar locations I timed most aspects of my travel to the minute. At home I knew what time to leave for the airport and cover associated miscellaneous administration. I factored in travel-times to the airport with allowances for the time of day and the travel peak queues. Generally, I was pretty accurate and only rarely would I need to rush to the gate or be the last to board. To achieve this I needed to make various allowances for all of the possible delay points; ten minutes for check-in, ten minutes watching someone argue with security, time for my own pat-down, the list went on and on. Some of these mandatory pauses held considerable scope for variation. Sometimes something would happen to threaten to blow my planning if it weren't for my fixation with a contingency allowance. Best case I'd get to relax with a coffee or a beer at some lounge and await my next pause, worst case I'd miss my flight. The reality was that between best and worst cases was a lot of waiting. My life on hold, waiting in urban desolation surrounded by people rushing, fast food and over-priced shops. I hated waiting anywhere, but airports are always the worst. At least on this occasion I was not in a rush.

I thought of my family and what they'd be doing at this time and considered calling them just to say hello and to share my news. I thought of what I'd say and how it would be received and decided that I'd wait until after I at least reached New York.

I was finally comfortably seated but a little restless in the airline lounge when head office rang. I welcomed the distraction as I'd been unable to settle with a book, newspaper, magazine, TV or even a movie, all of which I'd tried. They were very polite from the outset which made me suspicious, but I heard them out. They wanted to occupy my layover time and at first I made to decline the suggestion until their request tended to heavy grovelling. My time and space appreciation suggested that by the time I made a taxi trip anywhere I'd barely have enough time to make it back to the airport, but as their tone tended towards begging, I relented.

I was paged to the front desk as soon as I hung up the phone. I expected to be handed some background reading, faxed as a matter of urgency while I waited for the arrival of someone, but instead I was met by a well suited employee and a manila folder thick with reports. He ushered me to the tarmac via a long series of poorly signed corridors and ultimately to a waiting chopper.

I'd never taken a helicopter flight before, much less one of the corporate high flyer ilk. I enjoyed the feel of plush armchairs with a token lap-sash seatbelt tucked away, obviously little used. Clearly passengers on these aircraft were above fear for their mortality. Here was a form of transport which suited me.

As soon as we were airborne I was offered coffee by a woman dressed as a co-pilot. She asked suggestively if there was anything else that I might like, but I deferred my interest. Instead, I focussed on the papers in my folder, my background reading, periodically looking out the window to track my progress and the changing scenery far below.

The reading was not very flattering. 'My' company was under contract to turn around the fortunes of a potentially top tier company which was struggling. A familiar story of a market leader and innovator which had inexplicably lost its way and its place at the top; and so it's demise was all but assured. Perhaps the only thing that wasn't really familiar were the dollar figures involved. Until this particular trip I'd been a relatively low end consultant. Really, I was little more than a specialist monkey for which companies paid a premium for my specialisation. Often I would need to say only what my boss had briefed me to say and see what would have been evident with some fairly obvious research. My involvement with Emile's company was the anomaly in that they really required a big hitter that I typically wasn't and I felt renewed anger that I may well have been just a device to make someone else appear better. But that was the old me. My impact recently, the mark of the new me, was above and beyond everyone's expectations and clearly my company's expectation now, based on my reading, was that this customer needed a miracle. Based on my brief, a succinct footnote on the file, my company needed a phenomenal turn of fortune too. There was long list of very capable professionals who had tried and failed. Their reports were summarised with a fitting *mea culpa*. These were each legends in our domain-space who had found the task above them.

Perhaps had this been a public company then legislation for compliance would expose what was happening, but this was a private company which was haemorrhaging its future and no-one could understand why. Internal and external audits could not find the cause and now my company was tasking me with solving what had escaped everyone. I had until the end of the day to solve what had eluded others for years.

I suddenly doubted the reasons for my flight's apparently unscheduled detour. It just seemed too co-incidental that my company could be so desperate for someone of my capability to be here that an act of god or aircraft maintenance would make it happen.

Chapter - 13.

The Denver skyline was not particularly impressive. At night perhaps the addition of lights might have made my landing on a tower building more of an experience. But alas, my daylight landing only drew attention to my avoidance of the gridlocked morning peak-hour traffic at street level.

Several professionals met me on the roof, their ties pinned to prevent them flailing with the turbulent air of the slowing helicopter rotors. I walked tall and proud from the roof into a meeting room. Representatives of the client organisation introduced a pair of consultants from my own company, peers of the old me and fellow plebs of my boss; my team to use as I saw fit. We'd never worked together before but now they looked to cower in my presence; a mix of awe and fear. Given free rein to do as I pleased and to go where I wanted, there was no mistaking their expectation on my shoulders.

It wasn't until we locked ourselves in the room that my team shared the extent of their findings. What I'd initially interpreted as awe was in fact closer to sadness that they were sure to join the long list of failures and that I would share in their inevitable professional malignment. Today was the deadline for our company to turn around their business, and as they'd been on site continually for six months, their hopes of any remarkable epiphany in the next six hours was realistic.

I sensed their mortal concerns. The guy was a new parent and he'd not seen his newborn or wife for three months. My boss, also his boss had made the suggestion that his wife was welcome to visit, but also that such a visit would be interpreted as the height of unprofessionalism. He was damned if he did and damned if he didn't. I felt both sympathy and empathy for him. Overcommitted with a huge mortgage, the guy was terrified for how he'd feed his family and keep a roof over his head when he was cast adrift at the end of the day. Fearful, he'd effectively sold his soul to keep himself employed and now had no other options.

My other team member was more senior than me in that she had more tenure, but this was clearly not a point she wanted to dwell on. At least she was single, but this was sure to be a sore point. Her biological clock might have been ticking away but she was stuck from one appointment to the next, long hours and no opportunity to meet anyone, let alone the *'right'* person. If I'd been single, I would have found it near on impossible to meet anyone other than those who I worked with. If I'd needed such interaction to meet a soul-mate then the calibre of potential mates that this would avail didn't bear thinking about. I noted her lifeless eyes born of too much work and not enough life.

I suggested that we get out of the office for a coffee, but fresh air and Starbucks did little to relax my brethren. They kept looking at their watches, hinting at their growing concern that time was running out. I told them to give me their take on their task, their mission, apparently also now *my* mission. They each had a crystal clear picture of what was happening around them, even if they couldn't explain it. They both nervously fumbled a memory stick in their hands as if they'd been prepared to give a more formal presentation, but I wasn't interested in anything beyond a casual verbal brief. That they each had pictures on their phones of various key players spoke of their obsession and also of probably surreptitious surveillance. I studied the pictures as they summarised everything they knew. It took an hour for them each to divulge everything and ended with the guy shedding a tear out of stress. I sent him off for a milkshake in the sunshine.

The woman also needed a little time out too and I told her as much. She was a little hesitant but she left without too much coercion. I told them I'd meet them back at the office in an hour. Until then, my plan was to just allow my newfound brilliance to materialise something. I found a seat under a tree and I sat watching the world race by. I saw the pressure on people's faces and the weariness of their lives. I had the benefit of being only newly above their struggles such that I understood what they felt all too well, even if I was now above their worry.

I likened my perception to that of an out-of-body experience or perhaps the controller of a predator drone. I looked down on myself sitting there in my power suit, irradiated with a single broad ray of sunlight and noticed a man walking behind me outside of my earthly peripheral vision. There was a distinct scurry in his walk not unlike a mouse trying to pass behind a cat un-noticed. His behaviour drew my attention more than anyone else amid the crowds. I watched him slink along and blend into the pedestrian surrounds before I returned to my earthly body.

I followed him as unobtrusively as was possible dressed as I was and without any real intention of hiding my behaviour, following somewhere between an amateur and professional distance behind. A professional investigator would have found fault in my 'tail' but I wasn't so naive as to attempt to move from cover to cover or to peer from behind corners. I hoped that I looked like a man walking purposefully, potentially following only a path similar to someone or possibly anyone.

He, we, walked clear across town and the further we travelled the more interested I became. The guy was senior management from my client site; I recognised him from the photos my team had shown me. If there was a legitimate purpose in his jaunt he would have taken a cab. He wasn't showing fatigue at the prospect of exercise, but he wasn't dressed for a recreational walk either. Similarly, his gait didn't suggest a simple need for fresh air or to clear his head.

The way that he paused at the entry of a midrange hotel spoke volumes. He stopped and scanned his surrounds beyond simply looking over his shoulders. By good luck rather than good management I must have been outside of his area of focus on the other side of the street and I don't think he saw me. The guy was making sure he wasn't being followed. I knew I was witnessing an illicit rendezvous and I followed him inside for a better look.

I had my epiphany as I watched him at the main desk. My mind melded the detail that I'd read in the file on the helicopter flight and what my team had summarised and surmised. The penny really dropped when I saw two men and a woman march deliberately, three abreast across the foyer and meet my quarry. There was an odd mix of familiarity but contempt in their greeting before they all marched to the lifts. In particular, I noted the woman's face and remembered seeing her likeness in a trashy magazine in the airline lounge. In the tabloid picture she appeared to be deliberately in the background in a way that caught my eye. She wasn't a spectator in a crowd seeing a celebrity in the street, and she wasn't part of the celebrity's group proper. There was an odd ambiguity in her purpose. I vividly remembered that her face appeared adjacent to an article about the meteoric fall from grace and bankruptcy of a corporate high flyer was amazingly too coincidental. I felt like what I'd just seen in the hotel could have been a glimpse into a similar future magazine or news article. I wish I'd had a camera on me so I could have shared the event.

In 30 minutes I had two decidedly average lattés waiting before all four people exited the lift together. They walked in two pairs across the lobby; my guy and the woman close, but not intimately so, leading the other two. They stopped just shy of the automatic doors leading to the street. My guy kissed the woman on the cheek and then cordially shook hands with the other two, and then they all left.

I watched them go and deliberated my next course of action. My phone rang and on seeing that it was Emile I was surprised only that it was surely the early hours of the morning, his time. He asked about my progress and hinted that I should speak with him before I agreed to anything. That I was not yet in New York did not really surprise him, though whether this was on account of prior knowledge of my layover was anyone's guess. I was coy with the details but I said that I was about to make more waves. He laughed and offered a quip that my blue book value was potentially about to warrant another significant figure, another decimal place shift. I expected him to refine the details of his offer but instead he turned philosophical. He suggested that I use my time to consider what would make me happy. He didn't elaborate; he just left it at that.

No sooner had Emile's call ended that my phone rang again, this time from my team, more specifically from the woman. They were keen, desperate really, for me to impart my wisdom. I sent them on an errand to purchase a magazine.

Chapter - 14.

There was defeat in the eyes of my team on my return. I could see that they were deflated considerably more than at our last meeting. They were beaten. The guy was surely considering how he'd explain his failings to his wife and wondering how his children would look him in the face when they were cast onto the street for defaulting on their mortgage. That's what I would have been doing; that's what I'd done on the occasions when my boss would let me dwell on my mistakes until I'd supplicate to her to keep my job . That I ever worried like that was a very recent but still distant memory. Technically I was now unemployed but I didn't have a care in the world and I wished that I could grant others some of my confidence.

The woman looked at me with disappointment. I recognised the look as clearly as if I was looking at myself in the past. She was desperate to say something but, rightly or wrongly, she was holding her tongue. When I asked her to share what was on her mind I saw the relief and resignation that she felt she had nothing to lose.

"Your visit was touted to be the equivalent of our client's 'white knight'. But, brave Sir Knight, I'm watching you and thinking that our company could have cut our losses before now," she seethed, her tone dripping with venom. "Fresh air and coffee is not what we need right now. What we need is a plan."

I let her vent, figuring she was probably sick of an all tongue diet having bitten it for so long. I saw her mood lift with the aggression of her tone. I smiled and saw her expression settle somewhat, expectant that she understood she might have overstepped a line.

I said nothing for a good few minutes while I flitted through their newly purchased magazine. When I felt the air of sedition rise until I could taste it, I pointed to the woman in the picture and oriented the page for them to see. "You don't need a plan. That time, your time, has passed. I'm here to effect change necessary to save this organisation." They struggled to understand the poignancy of my comment relative to the picture. I saw puzzlement and realised that these mortals lacked my acuity. It pained me, but I began to explain.

I summarised the financial state of the company, the major players and potential of the customer so clearly that I impressed even myself. I stopped short of describing them as naive or stupid; *they* were human. The problem was that they were bound by the constraints of a logical mind; they were following the money, following the people, following the future. I was not restrained by such mortal limitations and I'd assimilated their findings, the media, human behaviour and everything else with the throughput of a supercomputer. That I'd been drawn to follow that one person was yet another example of how I was functioning on a higher plane. I didn't waste any time theorising as to whether I would have made the same association had I not followed him, thereby enabling me to learn what I did. The same could have been said had I not read that particular magazine at the airport.

I spoke for thirteen minutes but it must have felt like longer to my team. I noted how slowly the second hand seemed to click around on the wall mounted clock and this gave rise to wonder as to how fast I was talking. My team were quiet, dumbstruck, and after a while I accepted that they needed me to repeat everything more slowly or maybe to allow them to replay their recording of my speech back in slow time. I dumbed down my explanation as succinctly as I could. "Blackmail," then I explained what I figured to be the pieces of the puzzle that they'd missed. Thereafter, I saw struggled sighs of understanding and exacerbated appreciation that they'd never have understood the whole picture on their own.

After looking at my watch I called New York but was sparing with the details other than to hail my chopper and for my connecting flight to magically materialise. I wasn't going to say more but then I saw the look on my team's faces. I saw the long hours playing on them, resentment turning to acceptance, all amid the perpetual threat of failure. They'd put their last hopes on an expectation that I might come to their salvation, but they now saw that I was going to save the day but not them. I didn't feel sorry for them so much as empathy for their plight. I hadn't saved them, only granted them a stay of execution which might only be temporary. They were on tenterhooks as to what our boss would do with them next.

I took my call up a notch while I had head office's attention and explained that the solution was greater than the identification of the problem. They needed to hand administrative control of the tactical and strategic direction of the customer management to people invested in their success but abstracted enough to be able to make the right decisions. I gave them names, identifying my team. There was a mixture of appreciation and some sadness in my team's faces that took me some time to place before I accepted that my sharing of the limelight didn't grant them any more of a life.

Then I added a post script referring to a little known policy. More correctly, the policy was little publicised and rarely enacted except by senior management rewarding themselves. That employees were entitled to an accompanied, all expenses paid sabbatical for prolonged periods of exceptional conduct was a small price to pay for what they'd achieved. A small holiday would not be worthy of any attention to speculators in our company's futures, but the negative press should they, we, not deliver to our customers' expectations was different. I heard the other end of the phone go quiet, surely either marvelling at the fact that I was even aware of the policy or quantifying the size of the resultant expense. I further clarified that the policy was clear in that the employee was entitled to be accompanied by immediate family, including children, and I saw my guy's eyes brighten. I sensed subtle appreciation in the woman's face too, but also that her gain was largely pyrrhic, essentially swapping one lonely hotel for another. Her face too brightened when I mentioned the precedent set by our global HR representative whereby 'family' was only loosely defined. To scrutinise any definition of 'family' was to expose the company's 18th century policy regarding same-sex relationships and extended family values. If she wanted to take a friend of any sex or even a relative could not be rejected on any grounds. I had them, but I didn't hear any acceptance on the phone, so I threatened to withhold the final consultative report until I received the authorisation codes for their travel. I hung up the phone mindful that my helicopter was sure to be close.

Then I saw it, a business card; my boss's business card. She had been here. Perhaps if I'd been more in tune with my animal instincts I would have sensed her having been here before me. In retrospect, the whole place had the makings of her virtual scent markings. The fear in the employees eyes, the expectation that she would deliver someone more capable to save the day and the persecution that was inevitable regardless of the outcome. Whether she was the solution herself or was the master of the solution was irrelevant. What was important was that she'd positioned herself as the saviour and she'd been here.

I felt a renewed sense of anger at her. She was riding my success but a step ahead. I saw the logic of what she was doing. She probably tried to solve the situation herself, just in case. Doing so would have represented a last minute victory and earn her the kudos that was now mine. Maybe she discovered or knew that the task was beyond her. Then it would occur to her that she could up-sell her involvement, demand her share of whatever praise I deserved from corporate and insist that she briefed me with those pieces of the puzzle that miraculously enabled me to steal the show. She was cunning. It would be hard or impossible for me to refute if it came to that. It would also demonstrate her managerial capabilities in a far better light than what Emile had exposed. On the assumption that she was to face internal review and scrutiny, this could mean the difference between censure for a localised lapse in judgement or her sacking for some integrity violation; in a corporate environment this was the universal failure.

She was smart. Credit where it was due, even my cynicism could not undermine her obvious capabilities, and here she was, a step ahead of me. Whether she was headed to head office to face the music or was playing out some last ditch ploy against me was unclear.

I felt it again. I felt the boost in my morale with just the thought that she might be in trouble, but that I might be there to see her demise pushed my mood into euphoria. I imagined being there to watch her fall into oblivion. Perhaps I'd even get to see her grovel, see her beg for another chance; try to get me to use my current notoriety to leverage some deal for her benefit. I pictured her pleading, first in private and then in front of senior management. But I knew it wouldn't be enough. My delight in watching her on the back foot would pass, as would the pleasure of the permanence of seeing her vacant desk, and the joy when I started to hear news about her hopefully struggling to get another job. Then what? Time would roll on, life and work would move on. Perhaps she'd get another job eventually. Chances are the bitch would fall on her feet and then what? I couldn't let that happen.

The surge in me continued, this time stronger than when I'd fantasised about being involved actively in her demise with Emile. That I'd be able to preside over her scrutiny was a given. In my current state of mind I knew all I'd have to do was ask and I'd be able to cast the deciding vote on her future. It would be up to me to decide whether I'd be content to be the bigger man, ask for her resignation or rub salt into the wounds and destroy her professionally. There was a certain nobility in this approach, sure, but it wasn't going to be enough.

I didn't want to be the bigger guy. I didn't want to be the judge, it was more like that I wanted to be the executioner. It was odd that I restricted my options to just these, but I attributed this to a lifetime of indoctrination. Revenge always came down to wanting to be the judge, being able to see the bigger picture, or to get active. Had Emile been with me I expect he would have renewed his philosophy about forgiveness. I wasn't interested then and more than ever, I wasn't interested now.

Chapter - 15.

Even with the chopper ride to miss the evening peak, by the time I made it to the airport I'd missed all of the flights that would have me arrive at a reasonable hour. I also had no intention of taking another overnight flight. While I had the power I wasn't going to continue with anything that was going to make my fatigue or my life worse. I asked for a mid-morning flight instead, something at a leisurely time, and made my way by shuttle to the nearest five-star hotel; I can't recall which. I fell asleep as soon as my head hit the pillow. I didn't stress, worry or dream. I just slept.

When I did eventually continue my journey, I took the opportunity on the flight to consider what Emile had said. I thought of what it would take to make me theirs. I'd not been shy in telling them, Emile and everyone else, that *their* efforts at coercion weren't good enough, but really I wasn't sure in myself what I was waiting on. What was the magic number or condition that might have me align myself hereafter? Nothing came to mind. It wasn't about money or any philosophical angst about whether I wanted to be bridled. It was that I genuinely didn't know what I wanted.

What was it that I was looking for? Money was certainly part of it; that went without saying, but after years of Judeo-Christian indoctrination I finally understood that money wasn't everything. It's not that I was at all interested in entry to heaven or any other eternal reward or afterlife. It just made me think about what motivated me.

Only the naive think that remuneration is all about money, but the reality is that I needed to put a figure on myself. The time alone however gave me a chance to consider my price. I figured that as a gun for hire my fee would need to be more than just an exorbitant salary. I conjured up a number that on its own could be perceived as obscene. I reasoned that senior management of the organisations I assisted were paid excessively to preside over the problems that I solved. By extension, my pay packet could reasonably be even higher. I also decided that this salary should amount to little more than a mere retainer; something to allow me to be described as being 'on staff'.

More importantly, I recognised that I was a brand unto myself and like the many celebrities and personalities who put their name to endorsements, I needed more control. I decided the way to ensure the best for my name was more than to just avail myself to the highest bidder. The best way was for every single involvement to be a separately negotiated contract over and above my retainer. There was to be a sliding scale; my presence, my involvement, my participation, my signature all had a price. If I needed to travel then I factored in accommodation standards, calibre of car with or without driver at my discretion, and even paid holiday to my choice of destination for one week for each three weeks travel. I knew someone would identify that clause and exploit it through seemingly endless travel being sanitised with whirlwind visits home. The addition of 'non-contiguous' to describe my travel effectively added months of leave to my already impressive package.

I felt I was ready.

By the time my flight landed, I assumed the dust was settling on my exploits in Denver. I would have been the sole topic of discussion at head office, not the flavour of the month or just the man of the moment. I imagined that the office would have been all abuzz at what I'd achieved and what the future might hold. I pictured senior management in a frenzy to gauge what would be necessary to entice me and getting the authority to actually make me an offer to secure me. Rightly or wrongly, I expected to be really 'received' on arrival. I hadn't bothered to think whether I felt I deserved fanfare, but I definitely expected more than to have no-one awaiting me, particularly after such an uneventful flight.

I figured the Upper East Side was where I belonged and took a cab uptown. I probably should have demanded a limo or maybe even a chopper ride but the truth was that I had no idea where I was going to stay and didn't want to limit my options to those with access to landing pads. At least the air would have been fresh in a limo, something that I doubted in a chopper through the New York pollution. I knew enough than to appreciate fresh air in a cab ride.

This taxi journey was no different in that the vehicle wasn't clean and odour free. The driver's name was probably Mohamed, but he introduced himself as 'Mode' which I gathered probably represented acceptance of the majority of Westerners failing to see 'Mohd' as an abbreviation when it appeared on his certificate of registration on the dashboard. He didn't overstep his mark or really look to engage me. He would have understood that his opportunity to speak to absolute strangers didn't make them any more likely to listen or take in anything he said.

For all I knew the cabbie may well have said to me the exact same things he offered to all his passengers. At least he didn't talk about the weather, religion or politics. He did, however, talk about his family. He told me about his wife and children, his plan for their future and his role to provide for their wellbeing. He was 'just' a Cabbie, by his own admission. He wasn't a nuclear physicist or doctor from overseas slumming it with some menial job while he worked on getting a green card. He loved his job and while he had many of the same struggles as me; mortgage, money, and boss, he wasn't burdened with his life. I envied him. I wanted some of that, but I wondered how much my ambition was going to get in the way. Not that I was any more ambitious than him, but clearly my ambition was differently directed. God knows where my ambition lay though, as I'd never even thought of myself as particularly driven. I recall thinking how lucky this taxi driver was as I reached the hotel of his recommendation and headed for a luxurious and lonely suite in my suit worth many multiples of his monthly take-home pay.

I checked in at the main desk. Some anonymous celebrity was staying in their premier room which ruled out the penthouse and second top floor for their entourage, so I had to accept the best they had on offer. The manager offered me several choices, but his recap of the features of each option didn't make any really stand out more than any other in terms of desirability. I rarely travel with cash, but on this occasion I happened to have some on me, and not just smaller notes for tipping. I slipped him a few big bills and asked for something beyond the typical sales spin and absolutely no references to *feng-shui*.

I gathered immediately from his smile that he was capable of rising above or stooping below his usual pitch. He still pocketed the cash, but he also gave me what I took to be his honest opinion. He understood that the 'best' was more than just the most expensive, so if I wasn't paying for the room just knowing which room would cost more didn't help. His choice would be the West side of the building, outlook over Central Park, that much was obvious. But he also understood that I'd have little use for the space offered by the large suites, that corner rooms typically just make for a weird layout, and that huge bathrooms mean amazingly little to heterosexual men. He handed over a room key card and called for the porter to bring my baggage.

Beyond the allure of its prime real estate location, this hotel was nothing particularly special, not the best I'd experienced or imagined and not the worst either, not by a long shot. It was adequate but with an expensive urban view; nothing more, nothing less. It was clean and there were no wayward condoms hidden under the sheets. When I had a shower the water drained away because there was no matted pubic hair to block the flow and there were no tape worms splashing around in the toilet to keep me awake at night. In spite of my travels *my* yardstick was still simple. I didn't demand a spa, over-size bed, hot and cold running concubines. No wonder the manager knew I'd like it.

My wife and kids would have loved the room, but I just dumped my baggage and settled in with ambivalence. I recognised my cynicism and thought about this point just as I did whenever I checked into a room. When I do get to travel with my wife, my family, they love how different it all is. I can see the excitement in their eyes; a mixture of novelty and experience and I wonder if there was ever a time when I wasn't so *laissez-faire* about it all. I can't remember when I ever met the suggestion of travel with anything but a sigh, but there must have been a time. There must have been a time when I unpacked my suitcase rather than just seeing that as another un-necessary minute when packing-up, or checked out the single use toiletries in the bathroom rather than seeing them as being inferior to those that I'd brought from home, in spite of the obvious appeal of being free. As ever, it made me think about what I was missing.

My body clock was in its' usual confused state. Between travel to the airport, actual travel time, time zone differences, and then travel from the airport on arrival, I'd lost the best part of the day. Still, I was appreciative that on this particular occasion I didn't have the additional overhead of immigration, customs and quarantine of international travel, especially since 9/11. Regardless, my decision to leave Denver at a reasonable time meant that my quick cross country jaunt had cost me most of the day.

It was approaching what would be meal time at home, but without anyone else to impose a schedule on me, I wasn't really sure what to do. Had I been tired, I guess I could have gone to bed early, but that would have been contrary to my usual jetlag prevention routine. The problem was that I also wasn't fatigued at all, so turning in particularly early for the night didn't really appeal.

Bored, I slumped myself on the bed and mindlessly cycled through the channels on the television. It was perhaps three times the size of my television at home, but that didn't make anything on offer appeal. I also considered going for a walk, but that wasn't what I needed. I imagined starting out as a stroll, doing the tourist things or even just wandering around the park, but I knew that my energy would turn my pace into a manic race.

Then I thought of the gym and considered a sweaty way to waste an hour. I found it worked just as well to overcome jetlag and also to expose just how unfit I'd become. At home I had the family to provide some physical exercise; playing with the kids, shopping, housework, yard maintenance, the list went on and on. Not that it was real exercise or anything to really make me fit, but the point is that when travelling I didn't even get that. Wake, eat, work, pause for food, continue work, break for the evening, food, drink, sleep. Repeat. This, after many hours of sitting still, strapped into a seat with no chance for any exercise beyond the regulation periodic leg stretches to absolve the airline of responsibility for deep vein thrombosis.

Perhaps if I'd gone to the hotel gym on this occasion I would have amazed myself; run some remarkable distance at the rate of an Olympian or pumped iron like I belonged at a beach, all without raising a sweat. I was higher functioning in my mind and had every reason to expect that my physical capabilities would be similarly enhanced. But I didn't feel like it and I saw the time as being perfect to think things through. Something had happened and I needed to be sure that I was seeing it in perspective. I needed to be clear on more than just the last few days.

I started thinking about my work. I'd fallen into my role what seemed like a career ago. Somehow those small inconsequential involvements in various tasks had provided experience which, in retrospect, provided a near perfect progression to management consultancy. I had exposure to a wide variety of businesses, problems, solutions, people and the financials of successful and failing organisations. This had happened while my employer too had evolved such that the job and business I'd joined years ago was now indistinguishable from their current incarnation. My boss had once been a peer in my career, but never a friend. We were always worlds apart but her professional growth had out-stripped mine by several orders of magnitude, as if she'd been on the fast-track while I was in a coma. Somewhere along the way she became my boss; willing do to all the things that I wasn't.

Looking back, I couldn't believe where the past had gone. Somehow amid the evolution of my role I'd ended up travelling more and more. Now at the whims of my boss, I barely noticed that I was no longer the vivacious young professional thrusting for the pursuit of greatness and corporate glory. Instead, I found myself struggling to meet her expectations no matter what I did. At first, her demands weren't too onerous but gradually they got more arduous on me and implicitly therefore more trying on my family. Perhaps only Lassie the dog really knew what it's like to succeed in one feat and then be expected to launch straight into another more challenging than the last, week after week, year after year. What my boss sold to management as 'inspired leadership' was in fact closer to professionally legitimised slavery.

Forever in search of the elusive work-life balance, every day I rationalised my choices through simple logic; whatever couldn't be put off needed to be top priority. It seemed reasonable and provided at least scope for me to achieve balance in the face of reality. The problem was that my approach was flawed in that it provided too much latitude for exploitation, particularly by my boss. If work came up against a family commitment, I lacked the confidence in my job security to support any decision in favour of my family. I blamed my boss. All it took was for her to raise her eyebrows or roll her eyes at my very suggestion that family take precedence over a professionally crucial opportunity. My heart would race and I'd accept the task while considering how my failure on the home front would be received.

My wife was initially the supportive partner, understanding of corporate advancement for the greater good of her husband and ultimately family. Gradually, she'd moved from carte-blanche acceptance into resentment. Money and paying the bills was now more essential with a huge mortgage and extra mouths to feed, clothe and entertain, but not that she would perpetually play second fiddle to the demands of my work.

Sometimes I pictured my boss's reaction if she were watching and listening to my wife's reaction to my announcement that I'd miss another event or week. I'm sure she'd be smiling or perhaps laughing at the power she could wield and I hated her for it. Often I'd lie awake at night wondering how I could reclaim some control in my life, invariably falling asleep after hours of stress at the futility of my predicament.

My boss got some obscure enjoyment out of watching her underlings struggle and fail, and failure was inevitable. If any of her team coped, she used this as an indication of capability for increased workload. She took delight in it too, as if it was a game to see just how far she could push her staff until they imploded with stress, admitted defeat and resigned, or became her un-yielding disciple with the disintegration of their own marriage. It had worked for her too and she'd won award after award for her ability to motivate staff and push the bounds of what was achievable from an ever diminishing resource pool. Fear and acceptance kept us compliant. Until now. Now I wasn't scared of her and she wasn't more valuable than me either. I had become a real asset and yet again I felt the surge of inner power. I allowed myself to revel in self-indulgence and hoped I'd be able to continue to think things through fully, but I didn't get the chance. Before too long the phone rang and I was invited to dinner.

Chapter - 16.

There was a moment when I caught a glimpse of the old me in the mirror while scanning the contents of my new suitcases and those elements that I'd bothered to hang in my room closet. Faced with a meeting over dinner, I would have spent an unreasonable amount of time, for a guy at least, wondering what to wear. I would have considered the version of me that I wanted to present; the professional, the arrogant all-knowing consultant, the 'I'm so good I don't need to try' ring-in. The list of my personas went on and on. I wondered which combination of my new clothes would present me in the best possible light and missed my wife's guidance on the matter. Only after I paused to define how I needed to present myself was I reminded that I didn't need to worry about such trivialities. This was the new me and I could appear naked, in a tuxedo or anything in between and my capabilities and qualities would shine through. That's not to say that the new me was above window dressing, I just knew I'd look perfect whatever I chose.

I took a cab to the restaurant. They offered me a ride, some limo service pickup, but I wasn't interested. I wanted and expected to be courted, but I didn't want to give any kind of indication that my acceptance was a *fait accompli*.

The restaurant was nice. A classic silver service meal; excellent service, good food and an aristocratic atmosphere, it had all the makings of a memorable evening. Typically, I guess people would remember their meal for the greater experience, not the food or any one thing alone and while the food wasn't overdone, the same couldn't be said about my dining companions. The head of the company and a woman, the conversation was laboured and un-friendly and ultimately it all made the meal forgettable despite the promise of the setting.

Their attempt at an offer to entice me just didn't cut it. After finishing my *après* dinner coffee, my yawn was surely born of time-zone confusion, but it was timely nonetheless. I watched the guy's face as he rounded out the offer and knew he was just feeling me out. He was serious about his commitment to me, but he only positioned a number, an inadequate number, and I was now beyond a purely fiscal honey-pot. I held back on my demands.

I stood from the table and just left. I figured this would explain more about what I thought of the offer than I could say. After I left, I saw the guy say something to the woman. She followed me, leaving him alone and I held the elevator door open making the assumption that she was following me rather than taking some other detour.

Elegantly dressed and obviously about thirty years younger than he was, I hadn't previously wondered whether she was his wife, girlfriend or mistress. I guess she could have been his daughter. In any case, she was only ever introduced by her first name and their occasional furtive contact hinted little as to the nature of their relationship than the fact that they were 'comfortable' with each other. I couldn't work out why she followed me either. It wasn't as if she spoke to me or even looked at me for the entire lift journey. Not above chivalry, I held the lift door open to allow her to exit first and watched her hips sway as she floated across the venue lobby effortlessly in a tight skirt and four inch heels. I stayed in the lift and watched her await the chauffeur and limo for the corporate car.

Kerbside, she turned to face me and appeared to think for a time before casually stepping back to me. I left the lift to meet her half way.

"I've been asked to offer you *'anything'* to encourage you to continue negotiations," she said cryptically.

"I'm not really interested," I claimed, my lie surely evident like the arousal in my trousers. I interpreted the comment as proof positive that she was more likely an escort than partner and this did little to alter my heart-rate. I would have taken her there had a limo full of prom-going teens not driven past at that moment. I paused to deliberate only the details of whether what I did would affect my bargaining power before taking her hand and heading to the car.

I guess I could have waited until we got where we were going; the anticipation alone was enough. She raised the privacy screen and lowered her dress straps over her shoulders to reveal her breasts. We sat, knees touching but otherwise apart, looking at each other in the ever-changing colours of neon signage as we drove who knows where.

"I'm not a prostitute, you know," she confided. "My husband just asked me to do this."

"So why would you agree?"

She said nothing at first, instead covering her breasts with her crossed arms, as if the question made her feel over-exposed. "I love my husband and I can see that this is what he wants."

"So what's in it for you, other than *his* happiness? Time with me will come and go, and surprisingly quickly," I offered in an effort to ground any expectations as to my sexual prowess.

"My husband and you both prostitute yourselves every day for the good of your family. I see this as being no different."

She was right. With my realisation I could have been noble, but any nobility was suppressed by my arousal. I thrust myself onto her and ultimately into her. Sex between two prostitutes seemed as wrong as murder between two soldiers in battle.

Deed done, she offered me an aperitif from the limo bar. I accepted some ambiguously average scotch and sat back, expectant of post-coital dialogue. Unsure as to the protocols for behaviour after having had sex with the spouse of senior management, I pretended to savour my drink until she spoke.

"So will you join us? Stay?"

I said I'd think about it, which was true. I could have speculated that the sex did not make me any more or less likely to consider the offer, but that would have undermined my appreciation for her efforts. But it did make me wonder where their efforts to entice me could go from here.

Chapter - 17.

I set my alarm to wake me at my normal time, just as I always did. It was my small ritual to remind me that wherever I was, this was normal. It might have helped me with my maintenance of a routine, but it didn't convince me that my status quo was in any way desirable. Even though there was nothing pressing me to get out of bed early, like everything else in my life, any upside in a sleep-in was sure to have an even stronger down-side. Sure, I could relax, switch off, re-charge, settle into my current time-zone and savour not being forced out of a deep sleep. God knows I deserved it, particularly after what had transpired over the preceding days, but I knew my wife wouldn't see it that way. If she rang and woke me, even if she'd managed some rudimentary time-zone arithmetic correctly, she would be immediately resentful. She would add this to her impressive list of the many and varied perks of my travel, despite my continual efforts to convince her otherwise.

Loneliness always sets in on about the third day; I knew it and braced myself for it. The hyperactivity of the first few days gives way to the emptiness and pointlessness of being away from home and of work then sleep and nothing else. As different as I'd been for the preceding few days, apparently I was not above the reality of my life.

I thought of home a lot normally. Thinking of what I was missing, whether I was being missed, what I was to do on my return and how everything I needed and wanted to do was going to be compressed into limited time before I was off again. I hated my life. More correctly, I hated that my life was just one failure after another and I saw it every time I even thought of my wife or kids. All this under the watchful, gleeful eyes of my boss.

I wondered how other people did it. I never watched TV much at home for a lack of time, but I did whenever I travelled, mainly for the noise. I watched the lawyers and police, forever at work until midnight and took solace in the familiarity. Their bosses however are always jovial and compliant or mean but stoic and always with the best interests of their staff at heart. Mine was neither.

The realisation that I still wasn't able to distance myself completely from my life, despite my altered state, occurred to me as I watched TV while I woke to the first rays of sunlight breaking and Central Park in early morning mist. I was watching cartoons of the morning programming and it made me think of home. Had I been at home I would have possibly been doing the same thing; cartoons amid the lunacy of the morning with a young family. Different breakfast requirements, some reluctant to get out of bed, others looking for their homework, and all amid the distraction of cartoons on the TV.

It was part of our home arrangement; I would get the rabble ready for school while my wife would enjoy an extra joyous few minutes in bed. I would bring her coffee, receive my kiss and try to maintain some order until she'd woken adequately to face the day. As I reclined on my king-size bed in yet another distant locale, I wondered what she was thinking now; if she missed me, the coffee or the relative harmony that I created from anarchy before she surfaced. I was long overdue for a phone call, to hear her voice, but I didn't call her. Perhaps I should have called, if only to tell her I was thinking of her.

It's amazing the things I noticed or missed when I was away, good and bad. At home I had my routine and I took comfort in this familiarity. That I was woken daily by morning cartoons or someone needing help with their breakfast was inconsequential or even annoying when it happened, but its absence is grounding. Now I was alone in my room without any immediate reason to get out of bed the sleep-in didn't appeal and it served to focus me. Seated on my bed, alone and without the familiar tussle of children at play or disgruntled teens fighting the necessity to wake for the day, I missed it all.

Suddenly, the fairy-tale package that I was considering positioning to my 'employer' to have me stay lacked appeal. I'd gone to bed clear with my expectations, but now I realised the hole in my package; that there was no *'whole'* in my package. Clearly, I still had some thinking to do in terms of what I really wanted.

I moved on from the potential for melancholy just in case doing so might drag me from my altered state into reality prematurely. I took a long shower and selected some more of my newly purchased casual wear. I didn't need to check my look in the mirror to know I looked great. I had a leisurely breakfast, technically 'brunch', picked a random direction and set off on foot, oblivious to the crowds who were probably just as numerous at that hour as any other. In the city that never sleeps, I felt at home in my opinion of myself. Where others might have seen capitalism gone wild, everywhere I looked I saw organisations in need of my unique capabilities. It made me think of the real world and my role in it.

I couldn't work out whether I was being allowed a little time to think or if my employer needed the time to authorise a better deal. Either way, I had a moment to myself and theoretically there was no downside in my enjoying it for what it was. Soon I discovered that time to think can be a dangerous thing.

Stephen Covey, the celebrated self-help guru and author of 'The Seven Habits of Highly Effective People' once remarked that no-one on their death-bed ever wished they'd spent more time at work. Forever the cynic, I'd always interpreted his intent with a fair degree of scepticism. Yes, I didn't want to spend any more time at work than was necessary, but reality somehow got in the way. As much as I wanted to spend time at home, putting my family first, work was necessary and it happened that my work required travel. It was all very well for Covey to make such remarks and then to sit back and watch the royalties roll in. He could play with his kids in his big house and periodically take them on a holiday doubling as a media tour. That wasn't going to happen for me, so to pay the mortgage I had to divide my time, my life. But my eyes were opening.

I didn't know whether I really wanted to play hard to get. In the time I'd had to think, I couldn't decide now where my priorities were. I could have done whatever I wanted in my current state but I was reluctant to waste it on the pursuit of mere professional gain. My current state gave me unlimited potential. Was I really going to use it for work? It seemed like such a waste. Steven Covey would approve of that much, but investing it in my home-life seemed equally wasteful, like having a nuclear arsenal and never using it.

As confident as I was, I wasn't so sure as to whether I was capable of re-aligning my skills into anything else. Einstein probably wasn't capable of turning to sculpture, and in any case I couldn't think of something else. I had no hobbies, no lifelong passions unrequited; my boss made sure I never had the time to even think about it. I'd never been allowed to think, *'if money wasn't an issue I'd take up floristry or sailing or skateboarding'*. If ever my mind had wandered into fantasy about winning the lottery, after being suppressed and indoctrinated by my boss I always assumed I'd still work, perhaps just not so diligently. If ever I'd shared this fantasy with my boss she would surely challenge any belief that I was even capable of working less conscientiously.

Even the thought of slipping my mind into idle was a stretch. I was too capable, higher functioning and my brain was a finely tuned machine such that while pondering my future I'd managed to solve many of the issues I knew were awaiting me on my return. I felt so remarkable that I bet I could have even predicted the lotto numbers, solved global warming or fabricated another religion if I'd wanted. Why would I spend that potential on just my crappy job?

That wasn't entirely true. I knew that there was nothing for me at work in continuing as I was. Even if I was to be made CEO or adding a few zeros to my package was not going to inspire me. I realised what I needed was a challenge.

I spent the entire day thinking; walking and thinking. I took in the skyscrapers and the architecture as I walked, but I was too in my own head to really enjoy it. My wife would have loved it, but she wasn't with me. It was yet another place I'd visited from her wish-list.

I half expected that my wanderings would see me in the right place and the right time for me to experience another moment of greatness. When I walked past a bank I anticipated my reaction to evidence of an armed holdup inside and how I might save the day. When I caught a whiff of smoke I looked for evidence of a fire and tuned my hearing for the muffled cries of help from an upper storey window and started to hyperventilate in anticipation of a daring rescue through a building engulfed in flames. I wondered whether I'd allow myself to be immortalised or just slip into the crowd content with my anonymity. Despite my near continual pre-emption and planning though, it never happened. My name or likeness was not going to appear on front page adjacent to the word 'hero'. I managed to convince myself that this was neither here nor there.

I found myself alone once again at dinner after a day wandering around the city. Here I was in one of the world's great cities, abounding in potential and surrounded by spirited people and opportunity, yet alone. With someone else paying I could have gone anywhere for a meal but the reality was that I was bored, and even as confident and capable as I was, I was still on my own. I could be anywhere in the world and yet still in the exact same situation; alone at dinner, far from home and living out of a suitcase.

This time I was in New York. It was a city I'd only been to a few times before, but everything was familiar, particularly being alone in a restaurant. I could always spot the business traveller in restaurants. Where the typically single or dateless might look comfortable on their own, the travellers are all noticeable by their laboured efforts to look occupied. Beit reading a book or with solitaire on a mobile phone, doing something is the universal effort to appear comfortable. Even the best book still makes them look like outcasts, and relentless fiddling with any device during mealtime makes them appear manic at best or like losers at worst.

Laughter and frivolity was everywhere except for the virtual ghettos of despair where the proprietor saw fit to put those like myself; fellow travellers or hopeless lonely-hearts. No wonder I so routinely over drink so I don't *feel* quite so isolated, or eat so fast that I'm quickly suffering indigestion in the soul-less confines of my hotel room. Or maybe both. Sometimes it's a miracle that any work gets done in the following morning. Duty free liquor waiting in the room often helps soothe my mood but it doesn't remove the thinking that spins into overdrive when there's nothing else to do. I opted for an early night, clearly searching for the upside in being able to lie in bed watching a huge TV.

I settled my mind and focused on the upside of being alone in my room and my bed. It felt good. There was nothing to do, no need to rush, no worry for what was going to crop up. I relaxed in bed, listening to those sounds of the city that the double glazing couldn't stop. I ordered a room service supper and nightcap, and shamelessly ogled the maid when she delivered it. Perhaps she was used to this kind of confident arrogance among the powerful. I could have taken her then, had I felt the need or the desire, but I was controlled enough to understand that there was no challenge in it.

Though I was aroused, professionally powerful, personally confident, socially arrogant and sexually capable, I could have done anything. I figured it was time to call my wife.

I started to consider time zones to work out what my family would be doing at this time, but I lost interest in doing so. I didn't really care what they were doing and naively expected that they would be appreciative for my call and my news, regardless of whether it was day or night.

My family were less accepting of the timing of my call than I expected. I hadn't noticed that it was the weekend and my call happened to be just as they were about to walk out the door. I felt the frustration in my wife's voice. Not only was she solo-parenting, again, but she knew that I expected their world to stop while I interrupted their routine. The call lasted for twenty nine seconds, during which time I got a brief recap of pressing news before the kids started sounding the car horn and my wife hung up, flustered.

I didn't get to share any of my news. For all they knew I was still in Asia, still stressed at work, still floundering, still me. I was oddly almost appreciative for not having to explain what had happened since last we'd spoken. It occurred to me that there was no simple way to describe what had happened and the implications were going to be even more difficult to put into plain English. Where to begin? My wife wouldn't care that I was in New York. What was important to her was that I wasn't at home. That I wasn't where she expected was less of a matter of geography than semantics. All my kids probably wanted to know was when I'd be home to kick the football, or play dolls or go for a picnic. I knew they were arguably more interested in what trinkets I'd bring them after this particular trip. The thought made me wonder how long I had until adolescent cynicism led them to treat my repeated absence with nothing but contempt.

It was then that I received a call from Emile and I sensed a motive in him from the moment I recognised his voice. He wasn't going to improve his offer, share words of wisdom or offer me advice this time. He wanted something and I cut to the chase to ask what it was.

"Your boss and I have issues," he stated.

"Ex-boss," I corrected. "So what do you care? I thought you'd already put her in her place."

"Yes and no, but it appears that she has a vindictive streak."

"I told you as much." Emile said nothing and I returned to wondering as to the purpose of the call. Eventually I had to ask. "What's she done?"

"That all depends on where and who you are."

"I'm not interested in riddles, Emile."

"If you were here it could be deemed sexual harassment, but internationally it's more likely that I'll face scrutiny for sexual assault."

"You're joking, surely?" I couldn't believe it.

"Sadly no. And actually I was thinking that you might be able to help."

Emile was someone else wanting to exploit me. At first I was somewhere between disappointed and offended, but the more I thought about it, the more I moved into acceptance. That he wanted something of me was no different than everyone else. Whether he wanted something for professional ends or dubious reasons too was irrelevant. All I told him was that I'd keep it in mind. I wasn't going to make any promises to anyone but myself. It was high time I started to concentrate on me.

When the phone rang again, I was annoyed that Emile would follow up his call so quickly to labour his point but it was my company; they wanted me to meet with them at head office in the morning.

Chapter - 18.

I felt her presence before I saw her. It wasn't that I smelled her perfume or saw evidence that she was nearby, but rather that I sensed the electrification of the air. I was escorted to the corporate boardroom but the door closed behind me without my escort following. I was left alone with my boss.

I didn't want it to come to this, but it was inevitable. Like Hitler, I didn't want the conflict but there was no way that I was going to get where I was going without some blood being spilled, literal or otherwise. The challenge, I guessed, was to limit the collateral damage. This was to be the measure of my success.

She momentarily looked at me and then returned to stirring her coffee, focussed on the rhythm of her actions, while I stood facing her, marvelling at the opportunity of a lifetime. I paced slowly around the table, the echo of each footstep exaggerating the confidence of my gait.

Face to face with her, I felt my anger bubble in the presence of the embodiment of all that was wrong with my life. Clearly my company figured a confrontation was expected, surely to be watched through some covert surveillance and they wanted to see what would happen. At first I wondered whether this event was purely for their amusement, or if they foresaw a greater benefit.

I felt like striking at her right there and then, physically or otherwise, but I was suddenly indecisive. It wasn't for a lack of feasible options, but rather the feeling that I could get away with anything and everything. Moreover, the real cause of my indecision was that I didn't even need to do it myself. I knew at just the very suggestion that my acceptance of their offer was conditional on her departure that it would probably happen. I could beat her without raising my voice, let alone my fist. I enjoyed a cocksure breath which inflated my chest to the limits of my fine tailored suit jacket. But that wasn't going to be enough. Regardless of whether she was made to understand that it was her or me, and the company wanted me, it wasn't going to be enough. No matter how they put it to her or even if I was the one to deliver the news, I didn't want to be merely the reason or the messenger. I wanted more.

For a time I considered asking for something to taint her professionally. Long after some initial bitter taste would linger, I wondered what would happen if she was rendered unemployable. That would be poetic. That the one who perpetually threatened, subtly, blacklisting me would herself be on the outer and unable to work would play on her. I'm sure I heard the unspoken appreciation of future generations who would never have to experience her managerial style. I warmed to the idea. Surely it wouldn't be hard to find, or fabricate, evidence to make it happen. As smart as she was, I doubted she would have kept herself able to withstand really committed scrutiny. Dodgy money, monetary lubrication to see us focus our efforts elsewhere, over-quoting; these were the obvious ones but there were sure to be others. She was capable of anything, and maybe if I knew where to look she could be tied to anything from racketeering to child prostitution. Done right, perhaps she could look forward to some jail time as well as the prospect of struggling to be even menially employed thereafter.

We'd been left alone in some generic meeting room and with the doors closed I felt like a gladiator in a fighting pit with my nemesis. Just the two of us, the way we each positioned ourselves at either end of the table made our surrounds feel better suited to a cage-fight. She and I said nothing until our coffees were consumed. I felt betrayed by my reaction to the bitterness of cheap coffee.

"I told them you wanted to sleep with me," she commented. It was just like her; curt, provocative and straight to the point.

"News to me."

"Then I told them it had happened."

"And they believed it?"

"Why wouldn't they? You're male, I'm your boss. Despite any short-lived change you've enjoyed over the past few days, you mirabilist, basic psychology and human instinct, male instinct, makes it plausible."

"Plausible, but I decline your offer," I tried a little deflection while making a mental note to investigate another word in the dictionary when next I got a chance. "Why?"

"You simply wanted to sleep your way to the top. For my temporary insanity and to keep you quiet I provided you inside information and this is what really accounts for your efforts of late."

"They wouldn't have believed that."

"Of course they would. They did."

She left the comment hanging with an arrogance I knew too well. Traditionally, I'd almost feared her self-assuredness. It was as if everything she said was almost prophetic, that either she knew it was going to happen or she expected that saying it would turn it into a reality, but now she'd met her match. I wondered if she was at all intimidated by my newfound ability to carry myself and was about to say something to demonstrate the strength of my conviction when the door to our conference room opened. A procession of the cream of the company joined us, gliding through the acrid air between my boss and I.

I finally understood what the business was doing in bringing us together. I'd assumed it was just because no pond is big enough for two big fish, so the company could only have one of us. Perhaps they could only afford one of us. I was a prize, but my boss had obviously touted herself as the original and best, the mentor of the prodigy. I wasn't there for when she'd presented her case, but I could imagine her performance. She was good at that kind of thing, really good. I'd seen her in action before and I'd spent my life trying to ensure that I wasn't on the receiving end. But my meteoric metamorphosis was still only short lived success. As sure of myself as I was, my boss still had tenure and years of documented success to her name. I'd assumed that my company couldn't choose between the two of us. The reality was that greed made them want to exploit two tools in their prime.

I was a little offended that the Chairman himself didn't make the company case. Some underling, surely an up and coming senior VP took the podium and presented their problem, carefully choreographed to an audio-visual presentation projected onto the wall-sized screen behind him. He spoke without pulling any punches, daring to be honest behind closed doors. Their problem was to be our task.

I'd heard of this job. It was like '*El Dorado*', the fabled lost city of gold that eluded all who sought it, all of whom lost their lives searching. That parallel might be a stretch, but the fact was that it was a professional holy grail. Rumours abounded of the power that might be wielded by whoever might solve this problem. Systemic, endemic graft and corruption made this an impossible task. I knew it; I was still a pragmatist, despite my newfound magical competencies.

That I didn't even know the organisation was a client spoke volumes of how my company had divided their commitment to the task. To advertise their involvement was to stake their reputation on satisfying the client's expectations fully. To participate under the guise of faceless independent consultants who could be re-embraced if successful carried less risk. When they failed, as was expected, independents could be cast aside. However, if they succeeded, corporate spin-doctors could quickly find the way to sell some fanciful story of a revolutionary new resourcing model, while the media and marketing departments would wring every last drop of goodness from positive attention for the company.

My company was desperate, arguably even more than the client. I didn't realise just how desperate until the Chairman spoke. He needed a win, and not just as the veritable captain of the sinking ship. With everything he said, those assembled at the table squirmed, clearly uncomfortable at having an outsider share in their dirty laundry. They should have known that a Management consultant is tuned to picking up on such cues. They should have known by now that someone of my calibre wouldn't let that kind of information go un-used.

I figured it was time to state my case. I dug deep, even for me, harnessing arrogance that I never knew I had. In reality, it wasn't so much 'stating my case' as stating my demands. I didn't sell myself, my capabilities, my successes or do anything to justify what was indisputably an impressive package. I even added a few things that occurred to me on the spur of the moment while I had the floor. When I'd finished, I didn't look for any concurrence or acknowledgement, I just sat.

Only the sound of my boss's chair being deliberately knocked against the table as she stood broke the silence of all those assembled, their mouths agape. I braced myself, expecting her to try to better my effort, but she didn't even try. Instead, she only offered some clichéd quote about commitment and offered an anecdote about her being in for the long haul and that this was just the latest *'opportunity'* that would inevitably feature positively in her next performance review. The bitch even looked at me while she spoke, not even bothering to spend the regulation 63% of her time focussed on the most senior person in the room. I thought she'd trumped me.

The Chairman was less impressed than I thought he'd be. He nodded to my boss and asked her to sit. Then it dawned on me; that was all that was required. She was the employee, and that she was to accept the assignment with good grace was little more than ass-kissing. What else could she do, other than turn down the *opportunity* with her resignation?

My price out in the open, the Chairman initially just looked at me. With his best poker face, I couldn't discern if he was doing the numbers in his head or coming up with the words to express his decision. And then he spoke.

"Come on board, come back, do this and you'll get everything you asked for, and more." He offered his hand as if to seal the deal.

Not one to believe any gentleman's agreement, with or without a handshake, I held back. "I'll expect signed contracts before I do anything."

Chapter - 19.

As soon as I boarded the flight to Johannesburg I thought of another few clauses that I'd forgotten to mention in my contract. I was in first class, obviously, but I hadn't bothered to check who was seated next to me. Clearly someone at the company had a sense of humour.

My boss, now my peer cum partner in this activity apparently, had spent the entire time we had waiting in the airline lounge going to great lengths to avoid eye contact with me. Each time I strayed a look her way I watched her divert her attention to anything else, all the while using her peripheral vision to keep an eye on me. The old me would have been intimidated, but not now. I wondered if the tables were reversed such that she was looking to gauge <u>my</u> next course of action.

My boss was equally unimpressed with our seating arrangement, but unlike me, she let it show. She ranted and complained while I just settled in for a flight along the longest possible axis of the Atlantic. Her reaction amused me no end too and I made sure she knew it, which only served to infuriate her still further. I found myself fantasising about her being ejected from the flight which gave rise to no end of possibilities. Would I clap and cheer, would she be tasered first and then stretchered off drooling and still convulsing? Perhaps she'd make some movement that an over-zealous, jetlagged air marshal would interpret as a draw for a weapon. If this assignment was a contest, I wondered if this would mean that I'd won by default or whether the test would be invalidated.

Had we not been in first class, she surely would have been removed from the aircraft after her performance. Expensive tickets clearly brought tolerance, not just leg room and better cabin service. Placated with personalised service, some calming words and a quantity of alcohol, she took her seat and accepted that we'd be spending the best part of the next 24 hours together. She settled, probably for no other reason than she appreciated, as had I, that it could have been worse. We were in first class in individual cocoon seats and provided the partition between our pair of seats remained in place there was no reason why we'd even need to see each other. If we'd been in coach then it would have been reasonable to expect that only one of us would survive the flight.

Once airborne, the flight attendants set about their task of keeping us quiet, liquored up and full to bursting point with food. I was relaxed and carefree and so didn't indulge as once I might have done. I held back, unlike my boss. I couldn't see her through the partition, but it wasn't hard to keep tabs on her drinking by the number of times the hostess returned with a drink.

I soon gathered that the bitch and the attendant were actually friends. I shouldn't have been surprised; even Stalin probably had some 'friends'. In that sense, the attendant might have been genuine or just professionally obligated to appear so. At a bare minimum, it was reasonable that they'd know each other, particularly given the amount of time that my boss spent travelling and the relentless pursuit of frequent flyer miles made us always try to use the same airline wherever possible. That significantly raised the odds that they'd have at least travelled together. After the meal service was complete, the attendant made herself comfortable using my boss's foot seat. The mood turned jovial and once again I felt the upwelling of hate inside me that was absent when I sensed my boss's stress.

I hated her. My wife and family hated her. Each time she laughed, particularly as her blood alcohol level rose, my thoughts returned to options for revenge. What to do? To do it myself or to get someone else to do it?   I knew it was only recreational thinking and that I'd never go through with it, but it whiled away some miles in the air more than any other available entertainment and relaxed me so that I could get a little sleep.

Chapter - 20.

Politically, the country we were heading to was an insignificant minnow on the world stage which only attracted widespread attention for relative changes in seemingly incessant social upheavals. That anyone knew about the country at all was surprising only for the fact that what was happening now or in recent history was no different to the last probably thousand years, perhaps more. Last week there'd been another coup to overthrow some despot who only months earlier had replaced another dictator. Until fifty years ago, the country's biggest claim to fame was its' contribution to the accepted definition of 'Civil war'; semantics dictated that apparently this was not really a civil war. It was a moot point. It didn't stop the region from being classified amongst the most dangerous places on the planet.

Below the surface, however, was a miracle of geography, geomorphology and plate tectonics. It didn't have vast mineral reserves of the industrial staples like Australia, but it didn't need to. Millions of years of earth movement and erosion, the natural world's equivalent of social upheaval, made available all of the precious elements and minerals, all in commercial quantities, many available nowhere else. The more they looked the more they discovered; vast un-tapped wealth, ripe for exploitation. Platinum, Rhodium, Cobalt. My recollection of high school chemistry was limited, but it seemed that every rare and prized commodity was available here, hidden from the world by a rugged landscape, thick jungles, a largely uneducated population and utter inaccessibility.

Johannesburg was just the first leg of our journey to get there. In ordinary terms, I would have described it as a long way out of our way, but as it happened it was the most acceptable route in offering a better than 50% chance of actually arriving. Given the preponderance for many of the regional airlines to crash into mountains or be hijacked, I preferred the detour rather than to take my chance with fate. I knew I was amazing, but I doubted I could fly or dodge bullets. Add to the mix years of cultural factionalism across various borders, our flight plan necessitated zigzagging across airspaces in accordance with the whims of the current political climate.

What seemed like every few hours, we'd arrive at another airport, each a little smaller than the last, and board another aircraft, each a little less serviceable than the last. Ever since Jo'Burg I'd joined the masses in very socialist, single class cabins. Sure I was seated at the front of the plane, but that was all. There was no escaping my seating companion, still by my side like an incessant reminder that we were a team. By the time jet powered aircraft were a distant memory, I began to theorise as to what was worse; an enormous German tourist on one side and her on the other on larger planes, or the imposed intimacy of being pressed together in some single-engine Cessna taking us direct to the rich heart of the country. I held off making my decision on that front until after we'd landed, primarily because some tropical low altitude turbulence made our last leg feel like it was going to be my last flight ever.

I felt a little out of place when we finally got off the aircraft and into the corrugated iron shed that constituted the terminal. Everyone was there to meet us. All of the company high rollers were there, and I recognised many of the faces in the background as being local Government power brokers. They were all there to meet us; the team that was going to put the country on the map, bring about the necessary cultural, business and procedural change to stabilise the reform to the region, and probably to a lesser extent to restore the wealth to the people. I'd been welcomed and greeted before, but just not on this scale. At least it was still daylight. Had my, our, arrival been at night I felt as if we would have been subjected to a fireworks display in our honour. Perhaps elsewhere there was to be a small scale coup to mark the occasion instead.

I was dressed appropriately in that I was neither over nor under dressed, even though my new linen suit was well crumpled from the journey. That I'd foreseen the need for a breathable fabric for the journey epitomised how I was going to appear better than my boss whose perspiration marks grew worse and more obvious with every minute, even with the air conditioning. Open necked shirts, ideally in a bright colour were clearly the order of the day, so in that respect at least I fitted in well for the group photo after I handed off my jacket to some awaiting pleib. Sure I was fairer than everyone else in the picture, but that I was male and dressed colourfully made it look like effortless cultural assimilation. My boss had to make quite an effort to not appear as my secretary. As testament to my apparent belief in her competence, I left her to it, to make her own mark in the crowd. When we were given some hastily reproduced hard-copy print of the photograph, a memento, I smiled when I noted that she was cut in half by her being forced to the extreme edge of the group. I was centre stage, the featured visitor, surrounded by dignitaries. I had arrived.

Wealth was apparent everywhere as we made our way to the office in our motorcade with police and military escort. It meant a slight change to their schedule for our arrival, the state dinner was going to need to be delayed, but they were impressed that I was so committed to purpose. I didn't need to freshen up or be distracted with free-time before doing what I came here for. I set no expectations as to what I wanted to achieve in what was sure to be a brief initial tour of the facility, but I figured it instilled in them a certain insight into my commitment. My boss tried to sell her intention to need to do more reading and background analysis in advance of task commencement proper, but I don't think anyone believed her. Nor did they care. In a country where women are for sexual relief, food preparation and child rearing, clearly she was going to have an uphill job ahead of her just to be noticed, regardless of whether there was any merit in her intentions. I left her to her agenda and made no comment, or even facial expression, as to the murmured questions of her role in the visit.

The state of the roads and infrastructure improved as we grew closer to wherever we were going. Close to the airport I saw the slums and cardboard homes by the roadside which billboards for large screen televisions could not obscure completely. But gradually the unsealed road became sealed, then wider, then divided. Initially, a trickle of people on the road, all on foot, looked similar to footage I'd seen of refugees, but the difference in this case was that they were heading in the same direction as us. The flow of people soon became a torrent. Whole families were travelling, bringing with them everything that they could. I felt the anticipation of all of these people, as if our destination was the promised-land, where wealth and opportunity abounded.

What looked like a construction site appeared, carved out of the jungle in a great valley surrounded by steep mountains an hour from the airport. It soon became apparent that the whole valley was just one great construction site; mines, ore processing facilities, hubs for the planned rail and road transport networks, administrative headquarters, logistics and the urbane infrastructure necessary to house, feed, entertain and service an ever burgeoning population. What impressed me the most was that 'ramshackle' did not apply. There was clear evidence of planning and the pursuit of a longer term vision, possibly an under-appreciated or unacknowledged legacy of one of my fore-runners.

The place was a hive of activity in every direction, and I slipped into a fantasy that I was being brought back to celebrate the success that followed in the wake of a prior visit. But I knew I'd never been here before, and based on the reading that I'd done on the plane I very quickly appreciated the superficiality of what I was seeing was what had perplexed everyone who'd tried previously. They'd come, they'd seen, and yet they couldn't fix the problem that was keeping this community, this country, advancing on unprecedented levels but on a virtual treadmill so that their net economic progress was actually in the red. It didn't make sense to the myriad of professionals and consultants who'd tried to solve the puzzle, to make a difference. If I'd really hoped that the answer was going to materialise for me, then I was in for a shock. At this point I didn't give in to the thought that my transformation had possibly come full circle. I just figured that if the answer had lain waiting to be realised for so long, then even in the best hands it was probably going to need the dust to settle on my arrival before coming to light.

Chapter - 21.

Even the best of formal dinners can get boring after a while and this one had all the makings of the familiar; lots of people, boring conversation, and a general inability for people to not focus on work. I knew that my dinner companions might not have adequate fluency in the English language to support a conversation at dinner, and talk of the weather and a mass of cultural clichés based on popular international media can only sustain a conversation just so far. No wonder alcohol flows like water at these things. I knew I'd end up judging the evening by how long it would take for me to lose my façade of interest while still appearing as the quintessential solver of problems.

I'd long since known that this is what set me apart from everyone else I work with, both at my usual office and any of the countless organisations I'd visited over the years. The 'me' at work was, at most, only half of me. Realistically, it was substantially less than half, but I could put on a display of professionalism that would make most think that I was determined to out-perform a whole team of ordinary mortals. Downplay the fact that I had a life and family, emphasise my commitment to this particular assignment, highlight my willingness to go over and above for the company, how I loved to travel. Simple. Sometimes I'd be so convincing that I'd worry for what my audience would say to my boss, and particularly what she'd demand of me afterwards to live up to the picture I'd painted of myself.

None of it was true of course. I figured that everyone expected a degree of exaggeration, particularly when alcohol was in the mix, but it was in these periodic performances which possibly made up for my borderline competencies and infrequent failures. But those days were behind me. Now I was achieving and it was so easy. It left me a little indecisive in that I didn't need to impress anyone during a pseudo-social event like this, and so what would I do? I considered feigning fatigue or some generic illness that would have me be able to sit the night out. I also considered being honest and just telling them that I didn't care enough to attend.

Then I thought of my boss and what the bitch would do with such an opportunity. That alone made me want to at least turn up to ensure I would outshine her. When I learned that she'd used her early return to the hotel to make some calls, surely to overplay her astute insight, I knew I had to not only attend, but also rise above my usual efforts. I figured it was going to be simple. I knew it was going to be enjoyable. I decided to wear my red suit to mark the occasion.

If I was a gambling man, I would have put money on the likelihood of me sitting next to her at dinner. Someone would consider it appropriate that she would prefer to sit near someone she knew, particularly with her being a woman. I didn't want to sully any perceptions of myself by having a polite word to the organiser to change any seating plan. I resigned myself to whatever might be, especially when I saw the grand table was square and not the usual rectangular shape. Without wanting to shout, I'd be reduced to conversing with her and only one other person, surely the head of their organisation or possibly the leader of the country. It was going to be a great opportunity for me.

For what seemed like the first time in days, I was wrong in my expectations of the dinner and the role that *she* would play in it. Far from being forced to sit next to her, I was actually seated directly opposite from her. It made sense when I thought about it; I'd been picked as the brains of the operation and everybody wanted a piece of me. By pushing her to the background they could put someone of their choosing on either side of me. I braced myself for a whiplash injury over the course of the evening as I tried to divide my time between the president of the company and their principal investor. At first I smiled when I saw that she only had some youngsters around her, possibly the next generation of leadership for the company or someone's children. I would have ringside seats as she played nursemaid and got to watch me dispel any hope that she'd come away from the event looking better than me.

Within the first few minutes of being seated I realised that I would have really preferred a rectangular table, at least that way I wouldn't need to see her. No matter who I spoke to, who engaged me, I could see her. If I surveyed the entire crowd then I couldn't ignore her. Even if those on my left or right wanted to converse more directly, looking straight at them I could still see her in my peripheral vision.

I hated her. My amazing intellectual metamorphosis was suddenly replicated to each of my mortal senses and it worked against me. I could see her with crystal clarity, even in the low light of real candled candelabra. I could hear every word she said and the manner with which she entertained everyone. I could taste the acceptance in the air and how she was reclaiming ground on me with every moment she got in the spotlight. Worst of all, I could smell the pheromones of her sexuality fused with the animal scent of her expectation of the kill. I felt my heart palpitate at the confusion of my wanting to both damage and violate her.

I knew what she was doing; I'd done it myself for years. Demonstrate whimsical confidence to attract an audience, all the while drawing the crowd into a pliable, relaxed state, before slowly turning the tone to professional matters. Only when I knew I could say anything to my captive audience with unilateral acceptance would I exhibit the killing blows of my technique and share my thoughts and observations. I knew she was using my method. I also knew it was working.

I felt the balance of power shift her way and this just made my temporarily suppressed loathing bubble over to the point of distraction. I lost my focus and found myself getting drawn into her performance, the side-effect of which was that *my* seating companions too became her disciples.

I could have tried to reclaim my lead role, particularly as I felt it slip away, but I didn't. My inaction was not for reluctance, chivalry, carelessness or any other reason that required a decision on my part, but rather that my phone rang. I opted to answer it and leave the table rather than debate my future or fight the rising temptation for outright retaliation.

It was Emile and even before I sensed the desperation in his voice, time-zone analysis made it clear that something was up. Distracted as I was, I'd forgotten his earlier call. It seemed like such a long time ago, but time had not improved his predicament. He was now in big trouble.

At the very mention of her name, my boss, the source of his stress, I almost allowed myself to digress into a rant. Emile would be a good listener, an ally, and what's more I could trust him that what I wanted to say would be safe and wouldn't come back to haunt me. I held back only because it wasn't necessary; Emile beat me to it. He didn't have anywhere near the mileage in hating her as I did, but not only was it not a competition, he showed promise in his attitude. If this was a trait that I wanted to see fostered, I would have considered giving him top marks for the familiar mix of anger and an inability or reluctance to break the status quo for fear of the repercussions, except that Emile lacked a grasp of the concept of implications.

Chapter - 22.

Partially for want to distance myself from my boss, but mainly for a little additional privacy, I ventured outside into the evening, steamy with monsoonal anticipation. Emile was resentful at my efforts to silence him until we were away from the formalities. I didn't understand the exacerbation of his tone until he hinted that this was his only call and he didn't have all day. Only then did I fix the echoed, caged background noises to our conversation as belonging to some police station or law enforcement agency.

I also appreciated that the periodic muffling of his voice was possibly caused by someone, presumably a lawyer, periodically trying to temper or stifle what he was saying. Eventually, after increasingly frustrated outbursts not in English, I assumed not directed at me, I sensed that our conversation was not going to be interrupted further.

Emile asked if I'd thought about our last discussion. I knew this part of our dialogue was coming, but I hadn't planned my response just as I hadn't really considered his suggestion. I didn't need anyone else to provide any impetus to strike the blow against her for years of living in professional fear and domestic angst; angry, lonely, tired, figuratively castrated and mainly living out of a suitcase. If anyone was going to get her it was going to be me, my way, for my reasons. I didn't need or want anyone else's best interests at heart, or agenda at play, or even to consider their approach.

It was becoming clear to me that now was the time, here was the place, and I was the one. I was at my peak in every possible way imaginable. It had to be now. This task, that we were together, gave me the perfect opportunity to destroy her professionally and I was going to make it happen, mindful that whatever I touched would succeed.

I proudly shared the basics of my plan with Emile. To strike such a cutting blow to her professionally that she'd never work again, certainly in any related field or one that required her to assume any responsibility. Ideally I wanted to see her incapable of holding down any job thereafter, but I kept that detail to myself. That she'd do jail time for sure was to be the icing on the cake. I thought he'd be inordinately appreciative, particularly when I shared a dream I had of me waving to her as she was driven off in the rear of a police car amid a frenzy of media interest, but Emile didn't react as I expected.

He said something, a comment, but a nearby rumble of thunder drowned him out completely. I waited expectantly for him to repeat himself, hoping that his next words would come between the crack of some lightning and thud of the subsequent thunder.

"I want you to kill her."

Chapter - 23.

Emile's call gave me something to think about. While I'd hated her for years, traditionally I'd always held back for fear of the reprisals in my work or the presiding legal system. But over last few days my supressed hate had evolved. I was no longer settled into the status-quo, implicitly comfortable because I knew there was nothing I could do. Now I could see a way out, to achieve what I craved. Through focussing the new super-me, I could finally get back at her. What I wanted was not only plausible, but also reasonable. Dammit, I deserved to strike a blow against her for me, my family and possibly everyone else who would put me on a pedestal, such was how I imagined my actions would be received. But there was a significant misclose between my intent and Emile's.

I was not a religious man, not by any means. If my day to day actions coincided with the central tenets of any faith, let alone my religion as listed on my passport, then that was all good and well. The point is that I didn't moderate, temper or change any part of my behaviour to suit the wishes of my church or any other religion. I knew what was right and what was wrong, regardless of whether someone or any greater being would decree that I was destined for heaven, hell, nirvana, eternity on a spacecraft or re-incarnation as a dung-beetle. I knew I shouldn't lie, cheat, steal and generally I'd done the right thing. Until a few days ago I'd been faithful to my wife, and I'd certainly never killed anyone. While obviously I'd allowed myself a little latitude in the adultery department recently, there remained a pretty significant taboo in my mind about murder, in spite of my elevated consciousness. Even with the king tides of the ebb and flow of how much I hated her, I'd never considered actually taking her life. Purists might think me a hypocrite, but there was a huge difference between deliberately inflicting pain and deliberately ending her life. Admittedly I'd fantasised as to how I'd dance and sing when I learned of her demise at someone else's hand or through natural causes, but that was different. It wasn't even a matter of liability. It was that I understood the presence of a line which shouldn't be crossed, no matter for what I personally thought of her or how I figured others might rejoice if I was to do something.

I *could* have told Emile 'no way'. More to the point, I *should* have told him that his intent was not my style, but I didn't. I never got the chance after our call was cut short, truncated possibly by the electrical storm outside or by his desire to deliberately end the call on such a decisive suggestion. But I understood that I probably wouldn't have challenged him without at least conceding that I'd consider it.

Emile's closing request hung in the air like a fart in the shower. It got worse with time, before the taste started to clear and I got to appreciate the consequences, good and bad. I was obviously going to think about it, and soon enough I started to really consider it. Did I hate her enough? Could I do it? Could I get away with it? Without any hesitation, I knew the answer to these questions put the idea into the realm of achievable.

I actually spent more time wondering if I'd do it for Emile or myself, or theoretically for my peers as a kind of faceless act of community service before I realised that the question was moot. It was time and there was no time like the present.

I hated her and nothing of the last few days had improved my perception of her. If anything, I now thought less of her than I had a week ago. Previously, I'd accepted her treatment of me to be deserved on account of my perpetually flawed efforts to even try to appease a demanding job and a family at odds with the desires of my work. Now I realised it was that she had issues with me personally and not just professionally.

There was no coming back from this line of thought. I wasn't going to be this capable, this above my normal state and not exploit it. What was more, Emile's suggestion cum request meant that I didn't even need to suppress my thought processes as being born solely of self-interest. Sure I would benefit, but others would too. It might not have been a purely philanthropic approach, but I figured that all things done for a greater good had a basis of self-interest at heart.

I'd made a paradigm shift in my thinking and I barely noticed. I hadn't thought ahead as to whether I would later relish or regret my role, but there was no question of the inevitability of what I would do. I no longer wrestled with indecision borne of consideration of consequences, fear of persecution or moral question. I wondered more about what my thoughts said of me and that all it took was for the suggestion to be made by another that I accepted it without question. To me, this spoke volumes of how thin the veil over my suppressed anger was.

The only question was how. If it was going to happen, then how would I kill her? I allowed my mind to run amok, and focussed on a purpose countless options cycled through me for further assessment.

I hadn't previously thought of how many ways there were to kill someone. I soon realised that I needed some way to reduce the list of possibilities, but even this was an exercise unto itself. Did I want to make a statement? Not particularly, but this didn't necessarily render some methods inappropriate. In essence it actually kept my list of possible ways for me to perform this service as large and thereby didn't help.

Likelihood of completing the task and not getting caught too wasn't a particularly significant consideration. In other parts of the world, sure, but not here. I knew well positioned sums of cash would enable me to either slip the country un-noticed or have crucial evidence disappear, if it came to that.

The means of classifying the ways proved just as numerous as the ways themselves, largely because I didn't care. I didn't care if anyone knew, if she saw it coming, if it was actually me who did the deed or a third party, or even if it was done by hand, appliance, process or 'accident'.

Eventually I decided that in the interests of keeping it simple my preferred method needed only to not involve others and shouldn't sully my beautiful suit. Never the homemaker, I didn't want to contend with blood stains.

Chapter - 24.

I returned to the evening's entertainment focussed, but still a little unclear as to how to proceed. Everyone had adjourned to an adjacent room more suited to pre-drunken, relaxed conversation away from the formality expected implicitly with high table dining. No-one seemed particularly perturbed when I appeared at the door, which was just as well because I didn't feel any particular need to slip into the crowd covertly. I still had my phone in my hand and I figured that look on my face might have given the impression that I was considering another crisis in some other remote corner of the world that only I could solve. A drinks waiter brought me a beverage and I found a comfortable lounge for myself, on my own. There was no rush of people to join me and a less confident version of me, the old me, could have become concerned that I was being ignored.

I realised very quickly that I had been sidelined. My boss held court and had the entire crowd in the palm of her hand with an articulate mix of humour, anecdote, experience and socio-political satire. The laughter was punctuated with smiles of acceptance and nods of concurrence. When she offered some comment in what was more than likely the local dialect, I felt the whole room swell with cultural appreciation to such an extent that I wondered if the president was beginning to worry. He certainly smiled along with everyone assembled, but every popular dictator surely has a pleasant façade to hide what they were really thinking. I was struggling with my façade.

I didn't bother trying to smile or even to hide what I felt each time her eyes locked on mine periodically. Every single word she said grated against me, even though it wasn't directed at me. I hated the way she looked, the way she acted, the way she managed, everything about her. Even the way she spoke hit a nerve. That obscure words came up daily in her vocabulary, that she spoke slowly when she was making a point and the way she pronounced certain words; that when she said 'film' it sounded like 'fill-em' and how I could hear the letter 'H' in 'why'. It all made me want to punch her in the face.

I coughed and cleared my throat with the obnoxiousness of a geriatric tourist. I wanted eyes and ears on me, not her, and I was not prepared to edge onto her stage to draw everyone's full attention. Then I paused, took a half gargled drink of my bubbly, and sauntered through the crowd to an ice-sculpture of some bird, perhaps a phoenix, which I considered to be a fitting backdrop to what I would say.

In reality, I used the walk to allow exactly what I needed to say to materialise. It made for a very slow walk, and I knew I'd be pushing the limits of my capabilities, but I'd come to realise and expect that anything was possible.

I started with an assault on the crowd and their childish ability to be entertained with sideshow-like antics when there were issues at play to warrant our presence. I might have appeared a little petty in referring to my boss as an inconsequential but entertaining little monkey and half-witted accomplice in the same sentence, but it served its purpose. It made them face up to why we were here and that the exorbitant fee they were surely paying was for a service more professionally demanding than just post dinner conversation. It also confirmed me as the power-broker of the 'team', as if their recent fixation on my boss had distracted them on that front. I watched her slink into the background as she scowled at me, all the time shaking her head. I hoped that she wouldn't reduce herself to simply sneaking back to her room for a quick cry before composing herself. That was going to be the least of her concern.

I moved on to summarising the nature of the problem as I understood it and did a far better job than I'd heard my boss do between anecdotes which was probably only what she'd read on the flight. My recap included insight, observations from our post airport excursion, and displayed a depth of understanding that I figured a country desperate for change and help would want to hear. I didn't draw attention to myself so much as promise to share the source of the problem, and have in place the solution, by tomorrow noon. I was tempted to describe it as 'high noon'.

They were a tough crowd. I thought they'd share something or offer a cheer or applause or something to indicate that they'd bought into my assurance, or at least that they'd heard me. Instead, they took it as if my remark was a cue for the end of the evening. They each solemnly filed past heading for the door leaving their drinks and an ambivalent atmosphere behind.

The president of the country was the last to leave. He patted my shoulder as he passed, and with his back to me he started to talk, asking me to follow him to a more intimate ante-room. I couldn't help but think of the time I'd spent with Emile a few days earlier given the similarity of the setting, despite the cultural and geographic contrast. I figured he was going to share some 'old dog' wisdom about being too confident before I had all the facts, which was reasonable. He'd surely witnessed many of the prior consultants starting with a mixture of arrogance and spin that they were on the cusp of turning things around, or maybe they would try to extend their effort with a last ditch presentation. In any case, while he didn't put it past me for trying to start with a little expectation, he did suggest that I might want to temper my enthusiasm until I really knew what was going on.

I could have shrugged off his disbelief with some well-chosen but restrained words, but I was too good for that. To do so would have undermined everything about me, and most importantly it would also have sullied my professional reputation. After all, this job was going to be the making of my future. I wanted the inevitability of my success and then the subsequent realisation of that success to be what would be passed on to the media and professional organisations alike. I foresaw future generations learning about me as this country became the centre of attention. As I spoke, it occurred to me that *when* I succeeded, this was the stuff of legend that would see me in demand on speakers' tours, endorsements were probable … anything was a possibility. Far from this being just the defining moment in my professional life, it could end up being the event which charted the rest of my whole life. I wasn't going to end up on the scrap heap like the countless before me, exiled into isolation and never working again. The world was going to be my oyster.

I didn't let on that I still didn't know what was going on.

Chapter - 25.

The president, I just called him 'Sir', ended up tiring of the clichéd surrounds of a hotel bar that was a legacy of some bygone, colonial era. I hadn't said as much, but a room filled with 'great white hunter' souvenirs, animal heads and pith helmets had a distinctly tacky feel about it. It certainly didn't reflect a resource rich country with the potential to call the shots like the oil producing nations of the world had done for a century. He wanted to go somewhere we could talk.

For the first time since my arrival no-one spoke English near me as the hotel car and driver were made available to us. We sat together in the back-seat but this guy was far different to Emile and so I didn't expect conversation to flow effortlessly. It was reasonable that he wouldn't open up to me immediately, unprompted. I needed to remind myself that, as far as he was concerned, I was just the latest over-paid consultant being brought in to fix a problem. Until now I'd demonstrated only biting rhetoric, but nothing really substantial to warrant his granting me any more favour than each of my predecessors. Emile hadn't warmed to me immediately either. The president relaxed and ordered us each a glass of a strikingly mellow malt with an aftertaste of honey.

I expected our journey to be punctuated with him proudly pointing out noteworthy infrastructure or cultural attractions, but he said and did nothing, other than watch for any reaction I might make as I looked out of the window. By night, I made the same deductions of the city, and the country in general, as I'd done during the day, with the addition of the fact that the hyperactivity I'd seen earlier was not restricted to daylight. It was nearly midnight and despite the intermittent torrential rainfall, the place seemed just as busy now. I played my best poker face to hide any surprise or amusement in anything I saw, as if prostitutes, wild-animals for sale and a tented foreign exchange counter all on the same urban street corner was nothing that I hadn't seen before. It wasn't that much of an effort, but I saw more benefit in hiding my hand, particularly in light of the promise I'd made. Outwardly, I wanted to appear receptive to this as a purely social event while I bade my time until my great presentation to reveal all.

We stopped outside a decidedly average looking bar. Regardless of whatever cultural benchmark I chose, this was just a bar, but I kept my disappointment to myself. Emile's venues would maintain their place at the upper end of my expectations and by contrast, this place was going to blur into my memory of countless mid-city venues I'd visited in a multitude of cities across the world. Even my hopes that the décor inside would dazzle me after such an austere entrance were to no avail.

We sat in a corner, each to a stain-proof, faux-leather trendy armchair with a small drinks table between us. The less said about the drinks on offer the better. Even the drinks hostess was fully dressed which, to me, amounted to the final disappointment. The president looked like this venue was well below his standard, which was undoubtedly correct, but I held back from reminding him that it was his choice. I just sat, accepted my drink and pretended to take in the atmosphere.

When at last the president spoke, after listening to a tuxedoed piano man perform a few songs that may or may not have been from Billy Joel's repertoire, I was more than a little appreciative for the distraction. "What do you want?" He sized me up while looking at me through the scotch in his glass and between ice-cubes, all the while tumbling an unlit cigar in his left hand.

I smiled. "I probably only want what those before me wanted. The difference however, is that I'll succeed where they failed."

My comment amused him. I could tell from the way the porcelain veneers on his teeth were suddenly strikingly obvious adjacent to his black skin. "What's to say they failed?"

I hadn't thought ill of the guy until now, but his question made me think he was just another of the quasi-intellectuals who'd advanced beyond their capabilities and all reason through good breeding or circumstance that I'd met professionally over the years. Not that he needed to be liked, by me anyway, but he was just another asshole. In the past I'd needed to smile professionally, take a deep breath and compose a placative response; nothing to upset the customer. Those days, that attitude and concern for the customer above my own opinion were now long gone, but I stopped myself from sharing what I really thought of him, if only because I appreciated that wouldn't serve my purpose. I opted to just answer his question. "If they hadn't failed, I wouldn't be here."

"So what do you want?" he asked.

"I want to complete this job to get your country profitable."

"And what's in it for you?"

"Prestige," I joked, allowing myself to smile. "The ability to say in all professional circles that I'm better than everyone who's come and failed before me."

"That's an odd way to value yourself."

The guy was starting to annoy me. I decided to disclose a little. "I'm being handsomely remunerated too, but this will be the icing on the cake. I'll get more mileage and professional longevity from success where others failed."

I needed to bite my lip when he sighed in response, but I managed, only because he continued. "What's to say they failed?"

Cards on the table, I could feel myself being infuriated and when I remembered that I didn't need to hold back. I skulled the last of my drink and started. "Are you fucking deaf? Why would I be here at all if I didn't need to be here? I'm here because *I'll* sort out what the problem is."

"Do you watch 'Sixty Minutes'?" he asked calmly in reply to my escalated tone. "Even Sixty Minutes has identified that systemic graft is what's at play here."

"And you tolerate it?"

"Of course, and through my tolerance I've become particularly wealthy."

I now understood why the party had ended so abruptly after my grand announcement; everyone there was in on the arrangement so why would they want any outsider to arrogantly herald the end of their ride. I wished I'd been wearing a wire. His admission would make it simple for me to make good on any expectation on my shoulders or of my ego. "You can't possibly expect me to ignore that comment. Aren't you at all concerned that I'll bring you down?"

He shrugged again. "I haven't told you any more or less than I told your predecessors. You'll be no different."

"I'm not like the others," I said, determined to prove that we both had volumes of confidence at our disposal.

"True," he replied. "The others at least had a sense of priority."

"At the moment my priority is to the company that I represent. In serving them, I'll implicitly serve the people of your country."

"You, like the rest of those who come to this country are not interested in my people. But that aside, my point is that others had a worthwhile priority." He paused to make sure I was listening before adding, "You're just a whore."

I tried not to take offence at the comment. "So anyone who works is a whore?" I challenged.

"Only the ones who work un-necessarily."

Clearly I'd missed something. As astute as I'd been, I failed to appreciate the point he was making, albeit obscurely. "I would have thought you in particular would consider it *necessary* for me to succeed. All your people will benefit, and your regime will too with any improved stability."

"But will you?" he said.

"I'll be paid handsomely."

"Whore."

"Just being paid for my services doesn't make me a whore."

"True. That you'll simply move onto your next assignment is really what makes you the whore."

"It's what I do."

"It's just odd that all your obvious capabilities haven't taught you a sense of priority. You still think those who preceded you failed."

I couldn't for the life of me decipher what he meant.   I stood, sighed that I'd already finished my malt and left. I hailed a cab for the return trip to the hotel.

Chapter - 26.

Throughout history, the wisest of mankind have been able to recognise significant moments. Great minds might have prophesised them or seen them coming, or at least recognised them as turning points in history. Lesser minds have feared them as pre-cursors to the apocalypse, plague, famine, earthquake, pestilence, or even a technical occurrence to rival a catastrophic failure of the internet. Importantly, the lesser educated or ill-informed masses can't see beyond the cataclysm that will surely follow these moments.

I had likened my remarkable metamorphosis as if caused by the planets coming into alignment. I pictured the solar system, the diamond ring effect preceding the planets becoming perfectly in line with the sun. There was no warning, nor was a warning warranted. Higher functioning as I was, I classified myself as a great mind with respect to my recent change but in reality I was also a lesser mind in equal measure; I saw the poignancy of the moment but failed to look beyond. That the universe had taken millions, billions of years to achieve this milestone, it was naive of me not to foresee the inevitability of each planet continuing on their paths, thereby ending the remarkable event of their, apparently temporary, alignment. All that remained to be seen was whether my transformation would be permanent. I could dream.

The problem is that nothing lasts forever. Individuals, societies and whole civilisations have come to know or learn, and ultimately appreciate this for themselves. Even Neanderthals learnt that days of plenty preceded times of famine, and empires which had stood firm for hundreds of years all crumbled eventually. Whether the affected people believed it was of their doing or that they were pawns or victims of some greater universe or god didn't matter. Whether they had the metrics or wherewithal to be able to foresee when the end was coming was important only if they thought that it would end.

Perhaps no-one understands just how finite success really is as much as history's famous and infamous, particularly in their reluctance to stop riding the success of their heyday. Not surprisingly, few such great men and women die at their peak. The rest surely slide into mediocrity or obscurity, all the while hoping that their wealth or residual power will sustain or protect them before the universe regains control and drives its equilibrium. Once powerful will be seen as a threat, wealth will eventually turn to poverty, and the past will catch up with the present.

If I was honest, I knew it wouldn't last forever. Even the old me could have understood that much, so the new capable me had no excuse. I made my call to ride the good times for as long as it lasted and if I had my time again, I would have made the same decision. Faced with perpetual struggle and relentless looming failure, the lure of the veritable Midas touch was too appealing to ignore. However, in retrospect, I would definitely scrutinise my actions in line with my decision.

Even though whatever had happened to me came without warning, I naively expected some sign to precede a return to normality. I figured it was only fair. I didn't care whether anyone else should be able to see or recognise the forewarning or if it were visible just to me. All that was really important to me was that I would identify the sign for what it was and that my clarity would remain to be able to react appropriately.

My analogy of the planets coming into alignment was poignant. Had it happened 30 thousand years ago it would have been impossible to ignore. I pictured a primitive human, draped in animal skins venturing out of his cave and being in awe of what he was seeing. Even if it happened at night I reasoned that it would be just as visible, with circles of absent stars emphasising heavenly bodies in some kind of remarkable arrangement.

What I hadn't considered was what would be visible if my caveman had slept through the event or if cloud-cover had obscured part of the occurrence. Even if the alignment was visible and some ritual ensued, it was possible that they might awaken after a few days and note that it was all over, the end having occurred at some time, but that they'd missed the moment. The point is that they might note the start but be blissfully unaware of the end. I should have seen it coming, and if even there was no visible clue, then I should have anticipated it. Hindsight is a glorious thing.

That was the problem.

Chapter - 27.

My room was not empty when I returned. I was suspicious when I saw room service knocking at my door expecting me to be inside, but it wasn't unreasonable that someone might have ordered on my behalf. I was still in the corridor, ready to greet the waiter when I saw my door open from the inside. I thought for a moment that I'd confused my room or even floor for another, it wouldn't have been the first time, but on this occasion I'd made no mistake.

My boss was waiting for me in my room. She directed the waiter to leave the trolley and sent him on his way with a minimum of cordiality. I held the door open and allowed him to scurry past while she returned to her position on top of my bed.

Of all my fantasies over the years, this was not one of them. I hadn't thought of her naked or even scantily clad. I had periodically thought of how she'd receive my resignation if I ever was so brave, and wondered if she'd make some speech as to my departure in light of my contribution over the years or discredit me to my face. The point is that seeing her there wearing only a silken hotel gown was more likely to be the stuff of nightmares, not dreams.

She'd ordered a bottle of Champagne, and while seated on my bed she removed the cork and poured two glasses. I remember reeling at the poignancy of her choice, not so much that it was real French Champagne but rather that she was going to share it. Had she brought it *for* me, deferring to me, that would have been different, but she was doing it to share in my success. I didn't want to share anything with her, even though I hadn't succeeded, yet.

She had an agenda; I could tell just by looking at her. Seated on the bed, my bed, watching some in-house movie, she offered me a drink but said nothing. I tried to take her intrusion in my stride, but I couldn't vouch for whether I'd kept my alarm to myself or whether she was alert to my apprehension.

"What are you doing here?" I asked casually, determined to not sound threatened or threatening.

"The same as you," she replied. "We're a team in this, remember."

"Team bonding activities such as these are out of scope."

"We could bond very well. Think of the possibilities."

I struggled to swallow the rising vomit in my throat. It wasn't that she was ugly or anything, and she certainly had all the bits to make sex possible, but she was who she was. I had years of seeing her in my dreams and it was never quite in that way. In those visions she was the gremlin responsible for aircraft trouble which delayed a return flight, the dragon who slew the brave knight, the alien who popped out of my chest or the blood sucking vampire. She was never the object of my desire. She was the devil in a feminine form, and no matter how she tried to make herself look alluring, reclining suggestively on my bed, I could see her horns. I never thought that seeing her would moderate the hate bubbling over inside me, nor did it. Her presence actually served only to renew my commitment. I recognised that this was not only an opportunity to make it all happen, but it was *the* moment.

I wondered if she knew what I was thinking and planning, and if she did, what was she going to do about it. At a bare minimum, I hoped she would stop her futile attempt to entice me, but beyond that anything was possible. She might have seen the look in my eyes, understood in an instant what was going to happen and then beat a hasty retreat for the safety of another country. I was about to move to secure the door to prevent or slow her departure, just in case, when it struck me that this was decidedly unlikely. She'd never shied away from any confrontation to my knowledge and probably wouldn't even have it in her to slink away, even if I was visibly armed. If her reputation was anything to go on, it was more likely she'd have her own counter plan. Suddenly, I was worried.

I considered whether she might go pre-emptive and attack me rather than having a purely defensive plan. For all I knew there might have been a weapon hidden under the pillow. It didn't seem like her style, but not necessarily beyond her. Perhaps she didn't even need a weapon whether for offensive or defensive ends. She had a distinctly unlikeable personality and while it had surely evolved, the basics of what everyone hated about her must have been evident even as a child. She must have been hated all of her life and if I'd grown up being hated like that I know I would have probably wanted or needed to learn some self-defence skills. Being defensive was not in her nature and she would have wanted to strike first rather than wanting to learn how to defend against some first strike. She probably started learning Karate and its doctrinally sanctioned nobility and then saw greater merit in other more militant pursuits, possibly anything from Ninjitsu to street or cage fighting. I felt renewed concern for the feasibility of her tactically dealing with me as a threat.

"So what are you going to do then?" she said with unreasonably focussed, angry eyes. Her naked aggression surprised me until I realised that I must have been clenching a fist and gritting my teeth while I thought about her. My secret plan was out.

I didn't need to dignify her question with an answer, but it felt fitting to get her to demonstrate all of the qualities that made her so reviling to me. I didn't want to just kill her any more. I wanted to kill her and then some. "I'm going to perform a community service," I said arrogantly while I removed my suit jacket and hung it in the room closet.

She stayed on the bed, laying back into a mass of pillows with a cunning smile on her face. Expecting her to launch herself at me like a Ninja sprite, I scanned the room looking for something to bludgeon her with, but there was nothing readily at hand or even within reach at a stretch.

My body primed itself to perform. Wave after wave of adrenaline coursed through me. My breathing deepened and my heart pulsed such that I felt static electricity fizzle across all of my exposed skin. Everything I'd read about fight or flight was happening, except for one small but rapidly growing thing. I was aroused and so hard that I was suddenly apprehensive at the prospect of any scuffle that might require me to bend over as this was sure to be an impossibility. I hoped it wouldn't come to that.

I ignored my sexual readiness and stared her down.

I'd never thought of her as anything purely human as she was simply too evil, but I didn't really know what she was. If she'd shed her skin to reveal an entirely different life-form, I wouldn't have really been surprised, though I would have been just as ill prepared. I did get an inkling of what I was up against as she seemed to absorb the aggression that must have been seeping from my pores. With every second that we faced off I felt her sucking the life-force out of me.

I didn't expect her to be so lithe and fast. I'd read about black Mamba snakes being so fast that they could strike and withdraw without you even knowing that you'd been bitten, aside from puncture marks that seemed to appear from nowhere. That's pretty well how it was. Even replaying the event in my mind afterwards, I didn't see it coming. One moment she was staring at me, the next she had me immobilised on the bed, lying on my back with my arms awkwardly under me and forced upwards towards my shoulder blades. She sat on my chest and looked down at me, using her knees to prevent my elbows from moving.

I knew my legs were still free and I naïvely hoped that I might be able to perform some gymnastic act to regain the upper hand. I took a breath in anticipation of exertion and waited until I sensed for the right time to make my move. I needn't have bothered. When I wriggled my toes in eagerness for the opportunity, she leant forward and sliced her elbow across my windpipe so viciously that I lost my ability to concentrate on anything except breathing.

"What are you going to do now?" she asked.

Chapter - 28.

I couldn't see my watch and while there was sure to be a bedside or wall mounted clock somewhere in the room, I couldn't bring myself to look. Immobile from the waist up and too scared to move my legs for fear of having my throat crushed, I couldn't even tell how long I'd been in this position. I certainly couldn't gauge how long it was going to last.

With nothing else to do, I figured it was time to try to talk to her. "I doubt we could work together effectively now," I said.

"Like that was an option," she sneered without letting up on the pressure on my elbows. "I know how much you hate me, and I can only assume that deviant Emile has polluted your tiny mind further."

"He didn't suggest anything I wasn't thinking myself."

"So if I ease up on you, you'll do what?"

I cringed at the sound of the letter 'h' in 'what' and felt the surge of loathing and aggression from deep inside me, not that it did me any good. "Aside from the fact that I'm not entirely sure my arms are still functional, I don't rightly know. This is not how I planned it."

"I'll bet," she smiled like the bitch that she was. "Clearly you didn't vaticinate this, you poltroon."

I cringed at her use of more words I didn't understand. I closed my eyes so I didn't need to look up at her and tried to focus on options. It didn't help and really only served to emphasise how compromised my position was. I wriggled and tensed my thighs hopeful of a new opportunity. This was another mistake.

"What have we here?" she said, unexpectedly alert to my sexual readiness with my movement. "Surely you weren't going to try to kill me with that?"

I didn't know what to say or do. I attempted the same futile techniques I'd tried as a teenager when an un-warranted erection got me into trouble, but not surprisingly, nothing worked. Admittedly, my boss wasn't Bo Derek, not by a long shot, but she was still only scantily dressed and no matter what I thought, I couldn't redirect the blood-flow.

"It seems a pity to waste it," she reasoned.

I felt my eyes burst open with alarm but I was unable to speak. I was confident that my silence was a function of this as being a possible opportunity to escape her hold and not sexual opportunism. It had to be. *'Dear God'*, I thought, *'please let it not be a softening of my attitude to her.'*

I hoped there'd be a brief delay while she removed her underwear. This would be my chance. She'd be focused on penetration and would need to move to orient herself accordingly, she'd take her eyes off me, release my elbows and arms and this would be when I'd make my move. I glanced to the bedside table and saw not appliances, but a variety of potential weapons. A lamp, an ashtray, a telephone, a pencil and hotel stationery each took the form of something with offensive qualities. All had potential, though I reasoned that a paper-cut was probably not going to be enough.

But the bitch wasn't wearing underwear. I felt her fumble with my fly as she raised her gown marginally and slid backwards onto me. Pleasure and resentment without opportunity, all in one movement.

She raised and lowered herself on me in slow time. Her knees were now clear of my elbows, and with each movement I felt life returning to my previously trapped arms. I got brave. I removed my arms from under my body, my actions clearly visible to her, but I distracted her suspicion by grabbing her thighs.

I was evil. I felt evil, dirty and evil and I hated myself for it. I lay there looking at her as she straddled me, cautiously bouncing, her breasts increasingly exposed with each movement. She kept looking at me with a look of disdained power. She knew what she was doing and not just sexually. I'd lost interest in whether this was to be my last hurrah, but she clearly didn't share my concern. The bitch was still working to a plan.

I convinced myself that there was nothing pleasurable in the experience and it didn't take too much convincing. As I approached climax I hated myself still further for not being able to contain a purely biological function.

Job done, she leant forward to look at me more closely. I feared what she'd say to reduce my self-esteem still further. I figured she'd gloat that I couldn't complete the job that I'd come for and hoped that she wouldn't quip some pun to the effect that she was appreciative for the fact that I'd 'come', just the same.

She moved herself closer to my ear and I felt her hair drift across my face as she did so. She breathed in and I waited for the words that I'd end up remembering for whatever minutes I had left in my life. "Two things for you."

It was going to be worse than just one thing. The woman was going to escalate my loathing even at this eleventh hour. I waited and waited for what she'd say, all the while hoping that I'd be allowed to extricate myself from her.

"I'm ovulating and I have herpes."

Chapter - 29.

In the past, I'd felt many an upwelling in how much I'd hated that woman. Each surge would come and generally subside a little. I could probably have charted the level of hate in me if I'd ever cared enough to do so. Hate over time, I imagined that the graph would show little dips, lots of plateaux, notable spikes, but a definite upward trend. I could annotate the graph easily. Each of the few occasions when the level suggested that my attitude to her was softening it was more likely to be that she'd chosen not to air or publicise a mistake I'd made. I would have been so appreciative that I would have thought bad of myself for thinking ill of her when fully expecting her wrath. The reality of it was that she'd only filed the incident away for use at a later time; I knew this because she'd periodically remind me.

Those few periods where the graph levelled out were always based on periods of her absence; invariably secondments rather than vacations. Out of sight, she was rarely out of my mind, but sometimes she went off the grid through focus or geography and when I didn't get abusive emails or calls from her it was easy for how much I hated her to stay reasonably constant.

Being elsewhere when my second child was born, having my request for compassionate leave laughed at when my brother was critically injured in a car accident, being recalled mid-way through a long service leave vacation with my family in the South Pacific. These were just a few of the occasions which saw sharp changes in the gradient on my graph. There were hundreds of them, some more significant than others, but there was no escaping the sheer volume of increases relative to the infrequent falls and periodic flats.

I thought about how the current upwelling inside me would rate and appear on my chart. As my blood coursed, flooded with adrenaline and post-coital natural opiates, I quickly appreciated that the 'y-axis' of my chart was hopelessly inadequate. I knew that when charted, the spike between yesterday and today would show a rise like no other such that the preceding years would appear as a 'flat' zero. I knew it would appear much like a chart of wayward radiation from the Chernobyl plant; ups and downs before the incident paling into insignificance following the meltdown.

She removed her iPhone from the pocket of her gown and enabled the camera function with her thumb while she turned my head to one side with her other hand. She pressed her cheek against mine and stretched her arm with the camera so as to take a photo. "This one's for your wife."

I closed my eyes with the exaggerated 'click' and flash of the camera. She reviewed the photo and didn't like the screwed up look on my face. Apparently it warranted her thrusting a finger hard into my throat which took me by surprise and hurt so much that I thought I'd pass out with the pain.

"Eyes open this time you bastard. I want your wife to see the look in your eyes."

I briefly struggled an attempt to force the phone from her outstretched arm, but it didn't work. She just pushed more weight onto her own arm holding the camera which left her with, quite literally, the upper hand. But it did offer an opportunity. My arm was outstretched and within grasp of everything that was waiting on the bedside table.

With the click of the photo, I watched her orient the camera to check the resultant image. I don't think it was a particularly good photo, but clearly she considered it good enough. She smiled and looked at me with her gown covered breasts pressed tight against my chest.

She wasn't looking at my arm.

Chapter - 30.

I closed my eyes to keep the mental image fresh. I concentrated on the orientation of everything and the proximity of each relative to my outstretched fingers. Then I returned her look. All I needed was a slight distraction to buy me a few milliseconds. With her face so close to mine, I figured that just pursing my lips would be all that was necessary. She was not impressed.

I knew it was coming but felt as helpless as a chicken on a block awaiting the axe. It occurred to me that if a headless chicken can run around, presumably following some prior series of instructions, then the same approach might have merit for me. Expecting pain elsewhere in my body, I queued nervous impulses for my arms to respond with what I hoped would not be written off as a final great act of defiance.

I was oddly appreciative when I sensed both of her hands on my throat. I felt the pressure of those hands squeeze, thumbs forcing into my Adams apple, and hoped my arms would be able to act independent of any further guidance from me. I kept watching her, not wanting my eyes to betray me.

My outstretched hand was given only a basic intent; to strike with anything available. I figured that if the plan was any more complicated, then it might be more prone to failure, particularly as there was no time or scope for any ambiguity. As the pain in my neck grew more intense and my head went fuzzy from asphyxia, I hoped my hand would try for a cracked skull with the lamp rather than try for a slashing wound with a hotel envelope. My hand surprised me, choosing what I'd considered an unlikely weapon just as I lost consciousness.

Chapter - 31.

I don't know how long I was out for. I was wet, under-pressure and more than a little bewildered when I came to. My windpipe was still functional, just, and after I pushed her off me I found breathing considerably easier. Only then did I discover that the fluid on me was blood, hers not mine, and there was quite a volume of it too. I marvelled at the statistical unlikelihood of puncturing her carotid artery and broaching the spinal gap between C2 and C3 in one motion and wondered if the outcome would have been different had the pencil not been so sharp. I came to realise that my hand had independently succeeded with its one chance.

After a few good lung-fulls of air, I stood and looked at her lying prostrate on the parquet floor beside the bed. A near perfect circular puddle of blood surrounded her head, like a sinister halo. It didn't suit her. Even dead she looked like a bitch, admittedly with a HB pencil protruding from her neck. Needless to say, I didn't have any regrets that she was dead, but I didn't have the pride or sense of accomplishment that I thought I'd have. That in itself didn't worry me.

Content in as much as I could start a new chapter of my life without my boss, I took a long, hot shower, as much to remove her fluids from me as to freshen up. I felt clean, revived, renewed and full of promise.

All was good … until I wiped the steam from the mirror and saw my reflection. I was largely unmarked by her efforts, other than finger impressions still evident on my neck, but that wasn't the problem. Clear as day, I saw the old me. I was suddenly very scared.

In a daze with this revelation, I made my way back to my bed, tripping on her en-route for good measure. I sat on a corner of the bedspread that wasn't sodden and tried to think. My previous foresight and intuitiveness was gone, and the only clarity of perspective that I had was to accept that I was a long way from home and out of my depth.

Chapter - 32.

I knew she was dead, though I checked her vitals a few times, just to make sure. After sucking the blood from me for years, it seemed plausible that the normal rules surrounding reasonable fluid loss might not apply. She was dead, no doubt about it, but that didn't help me right now.

I tried to break down my predicament into small, do-able chunks, but even dead she was going to interfere with any well intentioned plan. Miracles were clearly possible, but I couldn't look forward dependent on another reoccurrence of my recent metamorphosis. That meant I needed to rely on the old me to work it out.

Could I still succeed on this task? Sure. A good sleep maybe and I'd fit the missing pieces of the puzzle; perhaps meet with the President again and this time record what he said to prove a case. It was possible. The biggest problem in the immediate term was that I now had a dead woman in my room and there was no escaping it. I was very fearful. My previous arrogant self-confidence was long gone.

I considered ringing my wife. If anything was the measure of the old me that was sure to be it. I didn't ring her when I was on top, and now I was considering ringing with bad news of a calibre that she would never have imagined. To give her credit, she wouldn't have seen it like that. She would have been supportive, but while I would have appreciated that support, I needed something more tangible. Nothing she could say or do from afar was going to help.

Emile was more likely to be a better option. I rang him and he was very appreciative. He shared of the extent of his worry and his relief at my news gave me a brief lift. He reiterated his offer, sweetened a little, but not to the extent that I'd positioned to my company. The funny thing was that I didn't care about his offer.

The mood of the call didn't change when I described my current predicament, but his concern didn't represent a solution. There was nothing he could do.

I was on my own.

Chapter - 33.

I decided to run. It was 1AM and I rang the front desk for details as to the first flight out, but there was a complication. Commercial airline schedules typically had a flight out at first light, but some civil disturbance in that flight's destination meant that the schedule was in complete disarray. It took a little time for the night staff to explain that the reality was that this meant that all flights were implicitly grounded. So was I.

I'd noticed the lack of highways and rail infrastructure from the air and at the time I attributed this to the geography. It struck me as being counter-productive to any progressive government wanting to setup their country for prosperity. Without it, there was no way of exploiting the untapped wealth as it was necessary for the minerals to go out and the money to come in. It dawned on me how easily the country was being controlled. Between state controlled media, internet access and even transportation, the President and his ilk were doing a better job than Hitler in the 1930's.

I could never prove that the turmoil over the border that was interfering with my chance of an exit was the doing of my new friend, the President. Whether it was or wasn't, it was done and by either bad fortune or bad management I was now locked into the service of this country just like I'd been stranded for purpose in Denver.

I swear I saw her eyes flicker and her face took on a look of a snicker, but on closer inspection she was definitely dead, still.

The room phone rang not long after. It was the President of the country wanting an update on my progress. I gathered that he'd been tipped off for my foiled intention to leave and so didn't attempt any ploy to mislead him otherwise. I only told him that I'd worked it all out and that I'd be happy to share my findings. He wanted to meet with me immediately. I suggested a location other than my room.

Chapter - 34.

The President was waiting for me in his car at the hotel entrance. I expected the guy to greet me properly, but he didn't even get out of the car. I joined him in the back seat but the car stayed idle and the driver was sent off for a cigarette.

"Have you learnt priority yet?" he asked. He looked me over in the low light of a cigar and the overflowing light from the hotel foyer. "And you've changed."

I'd assumed that what was so obvious to me wouldn't be noticed. Superficially, he could have been referring to the fact that I was now more casually dressed in jeans and an overpriced, collared t-shirt, but it wasn't paranoia that had me know otherwise. I tried to deflect his comment, "I couldn't sleep with my revelation."

His look turned disapproving. "Clearly not." He re-crossed his legs and butted out his cigar, "So please, tell me about what you *have* learned."

This was when I really noticed that I was back to normal. I needed to present myself like I'd never done before and I didn't have it in me. I felt the pressure of the moment and the burden of his leer and I was intimidated. I had no idea of what I needed to say, let alone how to sell it as if my future depended on it. I tried some oratory feint as if I just wanted to delay my answer, but he wasn't convinced and neither was I. It also didn't give me any more time to think or to compose words that just didn't want to flow.

"You know, I've met many of your kind over the years," he said. "They come driven with grand intentions and want to make their mark."

My yawn clearly annoyed him. It wasn't deliberate but rather was a function of fatigue and perhaps a little reluctance on my part to listen to anything even remotely philosophical.

He stared me down for a time before continuing once he was sure he had my attention again. "They come, wanting to prove a point, and that's the problem. They could save everyone the stress and the expense if they made the effort to establish their priorities."

"Would that have helped them succeed?" I asked, struggling to see the poignancy in the comment.

At this, the President smiled, his white teeth almost glowing. "You seem obsessed with their apparent failure."

"Maybe I just don't want to be like them," I proposed.

"That only proves your lack of priorities."

Had his comment been made indignantly, I don't know what I would have said or done. Instead, his words only made me think. I'd spoken the truth in that I didn't want to be like all of those who'd come before me. There must have been dozens of them, each disappearing into obscurity and never working again. They would have returned as failures, been professionally marginalised, and struggled to rebuild their lives at best. I didn't know any of them, but I pictured them choosing to live thereafter in self-imposed exile. They would have taken their families down with them, for better or worse, and I wondered what their wives and children would have made of the upheaval. One day they'd be living their lives, husband or dad periodically away and perpetually fatigued and stressed, the next cast adrift. Debts would go unpaid, they'd lose their home, possibly their marriage, certainly their sanity, and that would just be the start of it.

But the tone of the President's comment taunted me. I decided I had nothing to lose and even hoped that the pressure might see a break from my typical mediocrity. I took a deep breath and mustered all the authority I could harness. "On my return I'll have the world at my feet."

"Hmmm," he mumbled. "'World at your feet'. What does that mean?"

While I clearly didn't understand everything, I knew enough. I interpreted the question as his ever so subtle request for me to name my price. It had been my suspicion all along and this all but confirmed it, but I was still lacking in evidence. I was teasingly close to succeeding, on my own, and I felt my self-assurance rise accordingly. I wondered if my predecessors had got this far.

"So what's *your* price?" he asked.

There it was. Not so much proof as an explanation. All those who'd come before me had probably tried their best and then their failure was guaranteed by receiving their illicit payment. At this realisation, the flicker of confidence in me burned a little brighter and I figured I'd try to position his attempt to buy me as being futile. "You couldn't afford it."

"Look around you, my friend. This country can afford many things."

"Don't you think that money would be better spent on the country? On the people?"

"That is either remarkably noble or socialist of you," he said, the words clearly amusing him. "The fact is that the people of my country have no need for the wealth of your kind. Big houses and shiny cars and bank balances and business acumen mean nothing to people without education."

"So provide them that education," I insisted.

"That won't teach them priority.

That word again. Priority. Its continued use was beginning to annoy me, primarily because I was missing a point that was obviously so clear to him. I wondered if those who had failed earlier were taunted with this same word before they disappeared into oblivion, or even if they would be any clearer now, months or years after the event. I doubted it, even with unlimited time to think while they couldn't work, they'd never come to grips with that word, 'priority'.

"So what's *your* price?" he asked.

"Cash for complicity?"

"Call it what you like. Any price is worth it to teach you priority."

"You must appreciate that my current contract is a private concern, but it is impressive." I envisaged sitting back and waiting for him to start, name a figure, and then we'd massage the number until we reached some agreement. However, all the effort I'd put into thinking about my package while in New York wasn't going to help, neither would retrieving my copy of my contract from my room. Naming my price was going to be more than a little difficult. My contract was rooted in long term benefits and professional longevity, so it was non-trivial to apply any exchange rate for a one-time cash payment. If I'd never work again, then they'd need to pay, and if it was going to cost me my professional future, it was warranted. "My failure in this task won't come cheaply, you understand."

"Your priority is misaligned for this to be deemed failure," he taunted.

That word again. I noted it but did my best to ignore it and continued. "I probably won't be so easily bought," a surge of understanding had me lay the groundwork for my bargaining. "I have a family to consider."

"There it is. Your priority."

I glossed over his comment and thought more about the figure. Some mental arithmetic later I decided to mark my line in the sand with a number on par with and as obscene as I'd put to my company, but as a one-time payment; a big number multiplied by the number of years I'd surely never work again. I said it.

The President thought for a moment. "And can you see to the concurrence of your partner? What shall her remuneration requirements be?"

"I'm sure she'll be quiet," I began. I thought of saying more, but then the car phone rang.

Chapter - 35.

The President spoke in his own tongue. It's funny how difficult it can be to even get the gist of a conversation in some languages. I was an English speaker, though I'd studied a little French and German at high-school. I also knew half a dozen swear words in another handful of languages, the standard by-product of semi social hours drinking while travelling. From this exposure and a lot of listening to the efforts of a business translator I'd come to understand that there were a lot of similarities in the way people spoke. However, if the role of eye-contact and hand gestures are removed, and with an inability to hear or see the other party, as is the case while watching someone speak on a phone, it was all but impossible to even guess what they said.

Not surprisingly, I found a native language from the African continent to be nothing like any language I'd previously been exposed to. There were no obvious similarities of structure or dialogue, and really the only clue that I was the topic of conversation was in the way that the President's eyes periodically darted my way. I had to be content to wait until he shared the nature of the call.

To my untrained ear, the phone call did not end with any pleasantries, comments in closing or offers of continuation. Instead, the President just stopped talking. He sat with a grin on his face evident even in the interior light of the car while he cleared his throat, as if speaking in English was going to place different demands on his pharynx.

"That was my driver," he declared. "I now understand how it is that you could be sure that your partner would not interfere with any arrangement we made."

He looked at me, surely looking to gauge my reaction, but I'll bet I gave him nothing with my vacant stare and no heartbeat. He wouldn't have seen deflation, surprise or fear, and certainly not satisfaction or confidence. I suddenly felt the miles of distance from not only my home, but also my comfort zone. I made to say something, but no words came out. As it happened, I only shrugged. I hoped that the silence wouldn't drag on.

"You don't want to say something?" he asked while inspecting his fingernails. Given the dim lighting, I figured it was more a measure of arrogance than any real longing for a manicure.

I squeezed a last drop of fortitude. "Your contract was with me, not her, so I don't think I need to say anything." It was worth a try.

The President laboured a laugh. "Many would have assumed that a body in your room might at least reduce your price, particularly given your history with that woman."

"Her death was of natural causes. My price is my price." I didn't bother clarifying how he could have known of our history. It wasn't a secret and while I'd tolerated it for years and kept my angst largely to myself and my family, there was sure to be a trail, perhaps a drunken social networking comment. I wondered if that trail was particularly difficult to follow, and whether this was amongst the things discussed on his latest call or if he'd done his homework earlier.

He laughed again. "You amuse me. That much blood loss will inevitably lead to death by natural causes eventually, but typically the term 'natural causes' refers to deaths that don't require the involvement of another party."

"My price stands." I had nothing to lose.

"Alright then." He leaned forward and pushed open the car door as if to signal the end of our meeting. "I'll meet your price because I like you and because I'd like to see you focus on your priority."

I nodded and got out of the car, hiding my relief behind the façade of a laboured smile. The driver, obviously the President's spy, held the door as I left the vehicle. He deliberately stood in the way of me which I found annoying but tolerable. Even on my best day, which this clearly wasn't, I wouldn't bite at such a petty, testosterone fuelled provocation.

The President leaned forward to offer one more parting comment. "You might like to leave the country. All actions have consequences and the body in your room will only go so long before being discovered by someone less controllable than my own staff."

"It might help if your country was stable enough for commercial airlines to function. Between the country's instability and your control of all international travel I'm effectively stranded here."

"I'll make available my own aircraft to allow you to leave." He smiled ominously, white teeth almost glowing in the dark.

"What will that cost me?" I asked, substantially less confident than I'd been a moment earlier.

"Your fee."

Checkmate. The President broke into a deep belly-laugh which dragged on into shameless gloating. Had an appropriate rebuke come to mind and I'd said it, the guy wouldn't have heard it, but I was dumbstruck to silence. I waited for him to settle, but the time didn't provide me any great wisdom. The only thought I had was that I could still leave with what I knew. I could still bring the guy down when I got home.

Eventually the laughter subsided. He looked at me inciting a comment but I said nothing. "I'd say you've got a bargain," he smirked.

"What I know won't change by the time I get home," I mentioned defiantly. "If my silence isn't paid for, I could just as well bring you down when I get home."

"Yes, and your credibility will be shot by your subsequent indictment for murder."

"I'll just claim conspiracy. Your regime renders it both plausible and believable." I felt so far gone that words seemed possible without any direction from me.

"Needless to say that your sudden departure will do little to support your claim, or indeed your ability to deny the charge. Whatever you think of my country, extradition agreements are in place and we have a proud history of supporting independent and international policing efforts."

"We'll see." It was worth a try; my last gasp feint of self-assurance.

The President thought for a moment. "The fee you proposed is but a drop in the ocean compared to the wealth of my country and myself. Such wealth buys many things, and your silence can be guaranteed for much less than you'd imagine."

"Is that a threat?"

"Threat is such a bad word. Promise or suggestion is far more fitting."

I nodded in understanding, completely deflated.

"Gather your things. My driver will collect you in the morning."

Chapter - 36.

Something in me expected my boss to be sitting in bed on my return, nursing an injury possibly, but definitely very much alive. That she was dead was both a measure of her ability to inconvenience me, even in death, and also spoke of how my remarkable acuity and intuitiveness was now just a distant and fading memory.

Time alone in my room gave me a chance to take stock of my situation. I tried to not think about whether I could have done anything different over the last few days as that would have just depressed me into oblivion, but I couldn't help dwelling on how I knew all along that it was temporary. I paced around my room and fumbled my mobile phone in and out of my pocket with stress until eventually it dropped on the floor, its battery dislodging and separating with the force of the fall. Seeing annotations for the positive and negative terminals on the battery gave rise to an epiphany as I recalled my understanding of universal balance. At first, I took solace in likening my transformation to an additional cosmic charge which had now run down, returning me to the neutrality of normality. However, memory of electrical theory at high-school had me soon discount this analogy; the opposite of a positive charge was not a neutral charge but a negative one. I was suddenly mindful that balance would not be achieved in my simple return to normality. If I'd had my share of 'Yin', I could now expect an equivalent measure of 'Yang'. Normality was not as bad as it had once seemed.

I restored the battery in my phone and started to really stress at the prospect of a turn in my fortune. Like removing a first aid dressing, would it be better as a short sharp hit or a long drawn out affair? I didn't like the prospect of either.

The greater question was how this turn might materialise. I felt like a battlefield commander newly aware of his exposure and weaknesses on many fronts. Financially, morally, emotionally, physically; the list went on and on. I was susceptible to attack from every direction and any attempt to appreciate and negate the risk of each was going to prove insurmountable.

For all my gains of the last few days, my net worth and current bank balance was unchanged. I worried for a time at the idea that I might lose my job and how quickly my financial state would implode before I found another. Without my boss to sully my reputation, I guessed that I had a reasonable résumé and perhaps it wouldn't take too long for me to find something. Worst case, possibly the most likely case, was that I could be out of work for many months, and then have to start on a substantially lower peg and fight my way to where I was now, or had been. Losing the house was not just likely but an inevitability.

I couldn't escape from my moral failings everywhere I looked and crippling guilt set in very strongly. I felt guilty for all manner of my recent conduct. I thought of Fanny the air hostess and my adultery. I thought of my magnificently presented plans for Emile's company and what it really meant to the thousands of employees who were to be restructured out of their jobs. I'd never thought of myself as being a particularly moral man, but I was now a walking cliché for breaches of any and every moral code. Pride, lust, wrath, envy; I had pandered to each and it was more than I could handle. If these really were 'deadly sins', then I was sure to face judgement and punishment.

I'd long fought to rationalise my life and struggled. I'd teetered on the precipice of clinical depression for many years, but I'd always managed to keep myself from falling. Through the love of family, alcohol or sheer hard work I'd managed to keep it together, but all of that probably wasn't going to be enough in the face of an onslaught of adversity. I was sure to be an emotional wreck at the first blow and then having to contend with more.

Now at least I was physically unscathed, but I was still human, only human, and susceptible to injury and malaise just like everyone else. My wife and I had periodically commented that we'd been fortunate in terms of our health. We'd been spared serious illness, never had anything more than a minor bingle in our car, and even our parents were unreasonably fit for their ages. The good health of my family and I suddenly seemed precarious. I started to agonise as to whether my restoration of balance would see one or several of my family suffer with some agonisingly protracted terminal illness or sudden death, both of which ordinarily seemed to strike others but never us. It was more than likely psychosomatic but I felt itchiness in my loins and was reminded of my boss's parting gift. The turn had begun.

My thoughts were a scattered array of fear and pre-emptive responses, each trying to vie for focussed attention, but *en-masse* this was impossible. I tried to serialise each concern, naïvely hopeful that if considered one at a time they might be less ominous, but each seemed dependent on another such that they couldn't be separated.

Distant as I was with my rampant thoughts, it took some time for me to account for the vibration in my trouser pocket as being my phone and still longer for me to accept that making it stop was going to require my attention. The number wasn't familiar but I answered it anyway. It was head office and initially I thought that the CEO was after a progress report, but it soon became apparent that it was just some bean-counter wanting to account for some recent expenses on my card. It wasn't the first time I'd had to field this type of call and I started to frame a response, accounting for the varied nature and geography of the expenses as being purely for business need. In the past I'd largely direct the call to my boss and hope that she wouldn't want too much blood to sanction what she'd later describe as being of dubious corporate benefit, much like paying my salary. I did the same this time, demonstrating heartfelt confidence that my boss would not challenge any of the expenses, particularly in her current state.

However, my caller was not satisfied. The problem it seemed was that there were a myriad of expenses incurred on the card after my employment had been terminated. The word 'fraud' was used decisively and I looked at my boss once more lying on the floor with a pencil sticking out of her throat. I listened to my caller set a deadline for my reimbursing the expenses before the police were involved, all the while fighting to suppress my want to kick the lifeless body of my boss. Had the date he mentioned been one week or one year away was irrelevant given the dollar figure involved, even if I managed to keep my job. Only then did it dawn on me that, as my caller had pointed out, I didn't technically have a job even now. I spared a glance at my glorious suit and the rest of my recent purchases, each hanging perfectly pressed in the room wardrobe; it didn't seem worth it now.

I craved my newly absent competencies and it worried me, mainly because I knew it wouldn't help. Intelligence, confidence, arrogance, and an ability to sell myself wasn't going to carry me physically away from the mess I was now in.

I felt the gravity of my predicament. On the assumption that I made it back home, I was still screwed. I had no job, no nest-egg and no way that my employer was going to want me, not after how I'd positioned myself and still failed; I was the epitome of a liability. All those concerns were exacerbated by the realisation that my assumption was flawed and more than likely unreasonable. I'd killed someone and whether it was pre-meditated or in self-defence was a question for due process and little comfort. I half expected a knock on my door, the police possibly, something to end the stress of my wait.

I couldn't bring myself to ring home. The one person I should have been able to share my highs and lows with was there, completely oblivious. I did think about it though. I rehearsed the call many ways but I couldn't see it ending well no matter how I tried. She wasn't a fair weather friend, not by a long shot, and we'd been through a lot together. We'd shared ups and downs through our entire relationship, but nothing to rival this. It didn't seem fair to dump this on her; deep trouble of my own doing, when I'd effectively denied her the upside of what I had experienced.

I'd long described myself as having a keen sense of the retrospective. Some would call it hindsight, but in my case, I found that I only understood things of a personal nature sometime after the event. It was refreshing that the old me was still capable of this insight, even if I'd temporarily been capable of far more. Ordinarily I appreciated this insight, when it happened, tinged with a little regret that I didn't understand things at the time. Now, however, I hated myself for what I now felt.

I thought of my wife and family and I finally understood it from their side. My wife, holding the fort on her own, expecting me to return tomorrow or the next day after yet another trip, a brief time at home and then off again. Even when I was physically home I was elsewhere, none of which was what she wanted or signed up for. I thought of my children and all the moments I'd missed. First teeth, first steps, first days at school, ballet recitals, football games on the sideline, parent teacher interviews, family excursions and outings. My wife wanted a partner and my kids needed a father, and I'd denied them on the grounds of forced absenteeism. All my years of focusing on my work was so clearly misdirected. I couldn't bring myself to ring after coming to this realisation.

I was alone and lonely and I waited for the next blow of my new reality. It came in the form of a single call from home. It changed everything.

Chapter - 37.

My wife was clearly flustered. I sensed her heightened stress even before she uttered a syllable, but the fact that this was screamed was out of character. Prone to embellishment, my wife habitually exaggerated to prove her point. Over the years, 'the car is wrecked' had been used to describe an undeniably minor fender-bender, and 'there was blood everywhere' had incorrectly illustrated a scraped knee.

But the words 'is dead' is definitive no matter what the level of stress and I very quickly realised that this was not likely to be something blown out of proportion. I could sense her every strength was being directed into the passing of this message coherently, but I could only make out those two words as she failed emotionally, physically and most definitely verbally. My quick assessment of time zones told me that it was still daylight at home and my mind ran amok as I waited for my wife to compose herself enough to continue.

My wait dragged on for an eternity. My best attempt at consoling words did not meet their mark or serve their purpose across the divide of miles by telephone when physical contact, being there, was necessary. I craved details, to know more, all the while wondering how my return could be hastened.

I gathered that something had happened to one of our children and I couldn't help contemplation as to which child was involved, implicitly an assessment of which I'd prefer it to be. As a parent it's easy to have favourites; one who you prefer to be with at various times, but I say with all honesty that I love each the same, but differently. I love the feistiness of one, the easy-going nature of another and the heartfelt love for her father by the third. I found myself going through best and worst case scenarios and unwittingly I felt my stress rise with the tacit decision of who would I hate to lose more. I loathed myself for thinking it, but I stressed over it for a time before my wife became aware of her surrounds enough to continue. I didn't want to know if my worst fear was to be realised.

She got as far as mention of a speeding car outside our home when she broke down once more. The wait for her disclosure was unbearable and I hated her for it. I felt that if I was with her I'd be shaking her to tell me without the blubbing. More specifically, I knew had I been there I wouldn't be waiting for the news. Had I been there this accident, the details of which I was waiting on, would possibly not have happened. Had I been there, this wouldn't have happened and I would still be the father of three.

That I was now the father of none, living, came as an indescribable shock. I didn't mean to hang up on the call, but my phone battery gave up as soon as I heard those words that will remain with me forever. "They are all dead. Our babies are all dead."

Perhaps, surely, it is worse for a woman; for a mother to experience this degree of loss. I wouldn't know; I was born a male and I'll die a man, apparently a man with the misfortune of outliving each of his children in a single blow. I couldn't say what effect this might have on my wife; I could guess but I didn't *know*; I wasn't there. I wasn't there to hold her, to console, to share the intimacy of the grief, to protect her from herself if it came to it. I do know what effect it had on me though. I felt like I could write an omnibus to describe how I felt at that very moment and the seconds that followed, yet still I would die knowing that I'd never captured the moment, the loss, the sadness.

I'd heard that in the final seconds before your own death you get to re-live your life as a condensed series of memories all collated so that your final moments are unavoidably spent reminiscing in delight or regret. Perhaps the immediacy of the accident had denied my children their chance to capture the essence of their brief lives. Instead, it was me who got to experience those lost lives through the eyes of each child.

It took some time until I realised what was happening. It wasn't exactly as movies or my prior dreams had me expect in that seeing the world through another's eyes was more punishing than enjoyably cinematic. There was some reassurance only in so much as the fact that many of each of my children's featured memories were shared and I recognised that they would surely feature in my own pre-death re-cap. Special cuddles and hugs, crazy family moments, holidays, parties, and then all of the firsts; first steps to waiting parents with arms open wide, first days at school, first game of football. All those notable and seemingly inconsequential moments, now etched into memories.

I understood the finality of what I was experiencing, but it was too beautiful to be painful. It was a true gift from the universe or some greater divine being. Every glorious and happy moment serialised for my enjoyment in a way that no funeral service could ever capture. I felt I could die a happy man at the warmth which filled my soul. I hoped that my wife was experiencing the moment just as I was, naively thinking that it might help us in our grief.

Until the turn came. It hadn't occurred to me at the time, but in retrospect it was obvious that a life recalled would not all be good. I guess I was just so overwhelmed that it was easy for me to accept that a serialised recollection would feature the positives and the negatives combined into chronological order, but I was wrong. The benevolent universe had seen fit to separate the good and the bad and now I braced myself.

I saw all of my failings through the eyes of another, or more correctly, through three sets of eyes that weren't mine. I saw the school plays that I never made it to from the perspective of saddened eyes scanning the crowd of parents and not seeing Dad. I saw Dad waving goodbye from a taxi slowly outrunning a child on foot and a sibling on a bike. I saw Dad ruining the excitement of a family holiday with his disinterest in the mundanity of something as amazing as a flight on an airline and a stay in a hotel just like in the movies. I saw Dad asleep on the couch on a Saturday afternoon, too fatigued to do anything when there was fun to be had elsewhere. I saw Dad losing his temper over the slightest infringement of his wishes and his subsequent attempts to explain or account for his actions as being attributed to being busy at work or something equally as incomprehensible to a five year old. It went on and on and I hated myself for it.

When at last the visions ended, I thought of my family and of each of my children. I'd long since considered myself a failure, despite the shallow attempts of my wife to convince me otherwise which often only served to compound what I thought of myself. Now however, I *knew* I was a failure. I had failed each of my children individually and altogether. My best efforts simply weren't good enough. It was clear that what I thought was unlimited love and availability punctuated with obligations was being received as just disappointment.

Then it started again. A life re-lived, but a different life of which at first wasn't familiar. Then came faces that I'd seen in family albums or had described fondly by my wife; before my time but part of our shared history. I understood what I was experiencing. The first date, the first kiss, first intimacy, the ridiculous moments of being young and in love. All of the obvious moments were there including our wedding, the reaction to the first positive pregnancy test, the crossing of the thresh-hold in our first home, the first birth, and intermittent laughter at jokes and moments that no-one else would understand. I'd managed to enjoy the recollection of my children's lives without shedding a tear, but I couldn't help myself now. The tears flowed until dehydration became a concern.

As before, the good times ended and I waited like a child with his hand out awaiting some corporal punishment. I appreciated the way my wife's childhood was punctuated with lacklustre incidents only because it made me feel a little better, or more correctly, it made me feel that I wasn't the root of all evil. But soon enough, I began to feature; my inadequacies through her eyes. I started to take offense at how lop-sided her perception was until I accepted that now was not the time for me to challenge what was an undeniable gift. I saw her loneliness, her disappointment that I was never present and that I was never there, her frustration that I didn't 'get it'. The final frame of her re-capped life was through the coloured plastic of a bottle of pills through drunken fading eyes. The self-loathing in me bubbled over until I felt my clothing was stained.

Trashing my room didn't help, though it did offer a distraction for a time. Given the indestructibility of my room I did ponder a moment as to what had transpired there beforehand. The only thing that could be truly smashed was the television but countless viewings of 'Apocalypse Now' had taught me of the implications of careless TV destruction. Aside from that, I didn't think it would help. Everything I did to my room would be recoverable; it could be replaced or repaired, whereas my loss was both infinite and forever.

Crying didn't help either. What I needed was a drink to bathe away the misery of my current predicament and the prospect that more was likely, if not inevitable. I dressed in my over-priced but fabulous suit and left my room. I considered stomping on my boss's lifeless body, but I knew there was no point.

Chapter - 38.

I'd been a confident traveller for some time. I knew the traps, the tips, the tricks and the temptations. I hadn't seen it all, but I was worldly enough to have a reasonable expectation of everything. I was all too aware of the ploys by the scammers to prey on the tourists and the naïve. I hoped that this would be evident by my mere presence such that I would not need to be tested. If the early bird catches the worm, predators would need to stay up all night to catch me out.

But I was fatigued, deflated and depressed. I did what most in my predicament would have done. I went to a bar, the first non-hotel bar I could find. It took me significantly less than a minute, even in an unfamiliar town.

I threw my corporate card to the barman and started to drink. Out of habit, I began on the top shelf spirits but even as angry as I was I could taste that they had been watered down or similarly altered. Perhaps they'd swapped cheap product for the good stuff thinking that those who drank them wouldn't notice the difference. I poured my glass over the bar and complained briefly to the barman, 'Neil' according to the nametag hanging crooked on his much soiled tie. He shrugged, conceding nothing. Maybe by not challenging my accusation he figured he just might still get a tip out of me, or perhaps it was more that he genuinely didn't care. What he didn't realise was that I didn't care either, about his worthiness for a tip or anything else. I wanted to lose what was left of myself, but I just wasn't prepared to write myself off with anything.

The alcohol on the lower shelves wasn't any better. Eventually, I gave up on drinks which could be tampered with in favour of bottled beers. The only downside in drinking beverages of a lower alcohol level was that it was going to take a long time for me to be suitably anaesthetised. The minutes dragged on as I did my best to drown my sorrows, dancing the line between feeling euphoric with drunkenness and bloating from the sheer volume of consumption. I didn't want to pause long enough to relieve myself.

A woman seated at the bar approached me and wanted to share my table. She was the only other person there and I'd all but written her off as a prostitute except that her periodic banter with Neil the barman almost gave the impression that she was his girlfriend awaiting his shift end. I saw her watching me, not really caring what she did or thought. I was above fantasising for anything to appease my soul or my loins.

God knows what her name was. I let her join me for no real reason other than my want to vent a little in my alcoholically subdued state. In that she was a good listener. I let her speak a little of herself, and in turn I listened just enough to appreciate that she was a medical student.

The great thing about a medical student is the confidence she imparted in me. Would I have let anyone with a needle go anywhere near me outside of a hospital environment ordinarily? Of course not. I'm not stupid, in spite of my ordinary failings. That I even considered allowing it spoke volumes of my alcohol based attempt to suppress my emotional anguish, and also that it hadn't worked. So the offer from this nubile med student appealed. That she mightn't be a trainee doctor never crossed my mind. Why else would she have an array of meds ready in a clinical tool-box? I assumed that my story just hit a chord and she was offering me some pharmaceutical relief. I wondered if it would relieve both my grief and professional turmoil.

We left the bar bound for her room at some hotel and I felt my mood lighten, as if sex too was inevitable. I hadn't looked at her that way before, but there she was; female, proportioned and more than adequate for purpose. She wasn't of the ilk of some supermodel with finely honed features but I didn't care; I was still honest enough with myself to understand that I was no oil painting either.

As soon as we reached her room I gathered that sex was not going to factor into the equation. She'd never hinted that it was a possibility, but her body language suggested suddenly that it was definitely not going to happen. She turned focussed, clinical and professional and the shift in her demeanour made even the thought of sex seem inappropriate in much the same way that I always wanted to maintain the line in the relationship between my doctor and I.

My heart-rate actually settled a little, even with the appearance of the hypodermic needle. Gloves on, she looked like she knew what she was doing. She swabbed the injection site and cast the swab into the tiny bedside rubbish bin that typically only probably saw tissues and spent condoms.

I expected her to offer some calming words, if not for the needle but for her understanding of my stresses, but no words came. I assumed that she was in her professional element and as such to pander to any personal interest would undermine her role and probably Hippocratic Oath. There was almost a look of reluctance as she slid the needle in and squeezed the plunger slowly. I wondered for a time if she was having second thoughts or if she was concerned as to how she would account for some missing controlled drug.

I had on several occasions experienced pharmaceutical grade opiates when various operations entitled me to a limited period of sanctioned bliss. I remember the feeling of warmth flowing through my body and thereafter nothing seemed to matter. I remember at the time understanding why addicts persist, and now I looked forward to it. I waited for the same sensation to come and wash away everything even if just for a short while.

The hope of anticipation was only short-lived before it was replaced with abject fear. With the taste of marker pen in my throat came the memory of pre-operative anaesthetic. One. Two. Three. Four. I wasted four seconds until I even realised what was happening. The woman sensed the realisation that must have been evident on my face. Five. Six. Seven. Eight. I wondered if my blood alcohol level was going to expedite the inevitability of my unconsciousness or if I would last past the count of twelve as I'd managed the last time. I looked at her and asked why. I don't remember any sounds coming from my mouth, but presumably the look in my eyes said enough. I also don't remember hearing any reply to my subliminal question, but I vaguely recall the look in her eyes. Payday.

The microseconds of the last flicker of my consciousness dragged on, like a punishment unto itself. My eyes were long closed, but I felt the lucidity, warmth and life-force in me drain away. I remember feeling an emptiness unlike anything that I'd ever experienced, and feeling a frigidity at odds with the mammalian need to be warm blooded.

I hoped that my life had reached it's lowest ebb. More correctly, I wished that this was just a dream, a bad dream, and I wanted to wake now before I was confronted with anything else.

Chapter - 39.

I came to slowly with a dull but persistent thudding in my skull from the inside, and a periodic pain in my temple from what amounted to my head bouncing on the plane window with turbulence. I was cold and probably needed a blanket, but the hostess was too busy. I was still on my red-eye, we were landing, my ears were popping and the cabin was all aflutter with pre-landing routines from both passengers and crew. I'd missed breakfast and the implicit call for last drinks, and while my body craved non-alcoholic fluid of some description, the crew ignored me overtly. I was in a familiar place and no longer in any beguiling reverie.

I looked at my fellow passengers, particularly those beside me and smiled briefly at the confirmation that everything that I'd felt I'd experienced was nothing more than a dream. The greying Asian businessman on my immediate left was composed but looked to be annoyed. He scowled at me as I stretched, yawned and rubbed the sleep from my eyes. When I noticed the wet patch on the shoulder of his polo shirt, I felt a little embarrassed; clearly in my drunken sleep I'd used him as a pillow in alternation with the window. "Sorry," I said, offering repentant eye contact to support my apology as I pointed to his shirt. I kind of hoped that he didn't understand English or that he'd feign as much.

"Perhaps you should drink less," he offered with an English accent that defied his ethnic origins. "Then again, drool at least doesn't stain like tomato juice." He lifted a napkin from his lap unveiling evidence that my accidental drink spillage before I'd fallen asleep had impacted him as well. My embarrassment quickly turned to guilt and I grimaced, floundering for what to say in response.

The passenger on his other side, a rotund African gentleman, cleared his throat loudly and I hoped that he wasn't going to enter the mix that he too had been inconvenienced or splashed with juice. Thankfully, he had not made his vulgar noise to interject. He stopped fumbling a fat, unlit cigar and looked my way only long enough to fix his eyes on mine before slowly turning away with disdain and continuing with the cigar. He muttered something that made a younger, alert man beside him look forward to get a better look at me. I ignored his stares and faced the front, looking for a distraction in the airline magazine. I'd already read this dog-eared edition many times, just not on this particular flight. The featured articles were all too familiar; 'The untapped wealth of Africa' and 'a tour of New York on foot'.

Recognising my fellow passengers as surely the embodiment of Emile and the President from my fantasy, I took stock of what my dream meant. I looked beyond the superficiality of the fact that I was now wearing my old suit, the pants still horribly stained with tomato juice, and focussed on what I hoped to be the far more important point that I was still me, the same me. Work stresses superimposed on the realities of what made my life worthwhile. I wasn't going to win at work or at home the way I was going, and being here didn't progress either. Clearly, Emile was the voice of my conscience, good and bad, like a devil's advocate unconscious trying to show me what I was unable to see from day to day. I thought of my wife and kids and had the epiphany which had eluded me, particularly in my fantasised time with the president. Priority. My family were my priority, not my work.

I thought of my dreamed fixation of not wanting to be like those who had come and failed before me, particularly if it meant being paid out and unable to work ever again. My fear of such professional purgatory now seemed just so misplaced. Just how bad would it be if money wasn't an issue and I was forced to live out my days on a beach with my family, perhaps in the South Pacific somewhere? It did, however, make me wonder if the redundancies which I knew were coming in my company were something to embrace, not dread.

The revelations continued, serialised for me to understand easily in my hung-over state. The me in my dream was the same me, he had the same experiences and knowledge, just without the suppression of fear. Confidence, capability, competence, all at my disposal, all able to be directed to whatever I chose, I'd just chosen poorly. The more I looked, the more subtle morals I recognised, including the fact that Emile's son, the one who died, was me; a warning that I couldn't possibly continue as I was.

I worked it all out eventually, recognising all of the poignant clues that my sub-conscious was trying to tell me. It took me a while, but I finally understood my fixation on being a hero in New York which ultimately never eventuated. I didn't need to rescue a damsel in distress from a burning building or foil an armed holdup to be a hero, I could do that just by being the man I was inside, the husband and parent.

As soon as we landed I habitually flicked my BlackBerry from flight mode and was met with the subsequent inundation of reminders of pending appointments and email. I didn't bother reading them. That many of them were from my boss, surely threatening encouragement to not screw up, spoke volumes. She was just as I'd dreamed, except that she was still alive. That much was disappointing.

It dawned on me, however, that I had the upper hand. There was a depth to my experience and character which made me an integral part of her team and the company. She was crushing my spirit at her peril. If ever I garnered the self-assurance to challenge her, who knew what might happen. I didn't necessarily go so far as to interpret my dream as prophetic and that it was definitely time to have a physical confrontation; if anything my dream told me that wouldn't work out well. But living in fear wasn't going to help either.

Confrontation aside, changes were clearly necessary. I owed it to my family and myself to be the man I wanted to be, the husband my wife married and the father my kids needed and wanted. I could live with what I'd done professionally until now, but I had to be a different man from now on. And as I wasn't on my death bed, there was time. I knew what I needed to do.

First things first, I needed to travel less. If that meant needing to find a new job, then so be it. For all that my boss had done to quash my essence, she couldn't really control what others thought about me. If it came to pass that I did get fired, I suddenly had enough confidence to believe in myself and that I would find another job.

I smiled at my hostess in recognition when I saw her in the arrivals hall. Her name-tag told me that her name wasn't Faye, and her nickname probably wasn't Fanny either, but I didn't think to check. I watched her leave with the rest of her colleagues before my phone rang.

Caller-ID told me that it was my boss and I deliberated my options. I could answer it, or I could ignore it. If I answered it, what would I say? I saw the guy I'd slobbered over on the flight, and noted the annoyance on his face that I was prolonging the ringing. I let the call ring out, but she tried again immediately and my fellow passenger was displeased. My likening him to Emile made me think of what Emile had done to my boss in my dream. It made me smile.

"Can I help you with your phone?" he asked, intolerant with traveller's fatigue.

"Thank-you," I replied politely. "I don't need help." Just like Emile had said of me in my dream. He'd been right.

I decided to answer the call because I knew she'd keep trying. I took a deep breath and said two words that I hoped would mark a long overdue turning point in my life. I knew those words were necessary. Holding them in was helping no-one. It was time.

"I resign," I proclaimed with pride and conviction.

"Your comedic talents have limits," she replied unfazed.

"It's no joke, I resign," I repeated. I hadn't prepared what I'd say beyond what in my mind was a grand announcement.

"I have a problem with your statement. You'll note that I won't call it a decision, much less a well-conceived decision. Firstly, your comment comes at the commencement of an engagement which will be received as the pinnacle of unprofessionalism and rudeness. The customer won't accept it and neither will I. Secondly, this is something which needs to be done in person, so I'm not in any way comfortable in something as gutless as an over the phone resignation."

"I just figured it couldn't wait," I said, almost a little surprised that she would want to challenge me. "I thought you'd be happy."

Her laugh in reply was familiar. It was that arrogant, self-righteous noise which always preceded something unpleasant. 'Ha. Times are tough so you're going to take a pay cut.' 'Ha. I've arranged for you to go into a bird-flu quarantined region.'

"I take it you haven't read my emails yet, you moron."

I hadn't read them. I knew it was a stoning offence in her eyes, but I was a full 12 hours behind. Until now the best I'd managed to get away with was five hours; email was the last thing I did before I went to bed and the first thing I did in the morning. It appeared that I hadn't got away with it. Far from considering it a moot point given my resignation, I was apprehensive.

She sighed, long and slow. I heard the annoyance in her voice. "Had you read my email you would have known that I was to be your shadow in this activity." Quicker than I could appreciate her last comment, I felt her leer behind me. The call ended and I felt a tap on my shoulder.

"Don't kid yourself," she said as soon as I turned around. "If you want to take your chances in the big wide world, that's fine, but your resignation interview will need to be done in person. It's just going to be sooner than you anticipated."

I was taken aback a little, no question, but nowhere near as much previously I would have expected had I ever been so brazen to confront her. I was still standing, so I hadn't feinted, and while I could sense a little elevation in my blood pressure about my temple, that I still had a pulse was comforting.

"Excellent", I said. She knew it was a lie and I hated myself so much for even saying it that I felt like throwing up, but something was different. I was different. Clearly I wasn't as I'd been in my dream, but I wasn't terrified to the point of seizure either. I was somewhere between my normal self and how I'd fantasised. It was as if I'd seen and experienced the dark side and seen the error of my ways but was still mindful that there was still some middle ground to be found. I felt like the same person but there was an alien acuity and confidence about me. I knew she was staring at me and was aware of her breathing, but I wasn't intimidated.

"Good flight?" I asked benignly as I watched the luggage carousel. I saw she had her suitcase already and understood that she must have been in first or possibly business class. I knew it would give her the opportunity to gloat but it seemed the lesser of two evils to break the sour air and the silence of my wait for my suitcase.

"I was in first class, of course, away from the rest of you peasants."

I shrugged. To say anything was to buy into her power trip. More importantly, what she said was like the final instalment of my self-education; a lightning bolt of realisation between the eyes. What separated her from me was more than just that I had a family. She was evil to the core and I wasn't. That I lost sleep and stressed at what I'd done professionally was the measure of me as a man. I wasn't the heartless management consultant, she was, it was a key differentiator. Having experienced guilt for my conduct with my realisation in my dream, I didn't feel obliged to re-live it.

There was no banter between us for the entire trip to our hotel. We both sat in the backseat, me looking out the window and her fiddling with her blackberry. It wasn't pretty, but it wasn't bad. I felt strong purely by the fact that I wasn't cowering in her presence or similarly supplicating myself. Actually, the silence between us was glorious. I felt empowered by it just as I felt it eating away at her. She must have felt the playing field had been levelled; it felt obvious to me. I wondered if she was at a loss as to what to do about it. It made me smile that I was causing her a little angst.

The hotel was just how I'd dreamed; a fast check-in, but she went to her room and I went to mine. I showered, shaved and changed in quick time and met her again in the foyer.

We caught a taxi to the office of our client organisation. Only when we arrived on site did I think about what I was supposed to do. It warranted confirming her intentions as to what role she and I would play in proceedings. "So what would you like me to do if you are here too?"

"I'll do what needs to be done."

She said it with such faith that my feelings were a little hurt, but still I wasn't threatened. "What's to say I won't impress them, and you?"

She raised her eyebrows and looked at me. "There is nothing that you could possibly do to impress me. If you were at all capable of it, you would have done it by now surely."

I smiled at her knowing full well that it would not make her happy, but I didn't feel the groundswell of loathing that I'd imagined. I took her comment in my stride, not lowering myself to sink into any malevolence.

"You might be surprised," I said confidently. I kept the smile on my face as if I knew something she didn't.

Chapter - 40.

On our arrival on site my boss and I braced ourselves to be met with outright hostility; we could sense it as we approached. We walked together at first but, unlike me, she clearly fancied the confrontation so I settled in behind her for the last few steps to the score of management there to greet us. Oddly enough, there was a familiarity about the customer setting and group. I'd never actually been there before or met any of the people who greeted us politely, albeit with a measure of displeasure, but I knew the place and the people. My boss pushed me to the outer and shook the hand of the most senior person there but made the mistake of calling him Emile. Everyone assembled smiled but didn't correct her. I knew it wasn't Emile.

We settled into their boardroom and the customer re-iterated the problems that warranted my being there, our being there. One at a time they stood, presented their case and handed the baton-like laser pointer to their counterpart. I nodded as if I'd heard it all before, largely because I had. I didn't remember their names, but I remembered their voices and the disinterest with which they spoke, as if they'd gone through this rigmarole previously. They didn't want to explain their issues to outsiders, again. They certainly didn't want to air their dirty laundry to anyone who would just make recommendations with the obnoxiousness of their distraction like the consultants that we were. I understood them and held my tongue, even though I could have shared a plan which met the mark of senior management in my dream. I noted the appreciation in their eyes; that I was not the one to worry about.

My boss was at her best. She demonstrated all the traits that made her reviled, feared and avoided by everyone. I tried to distance myself from her as best I could, but that I said nothing while she did the verbal savaging wasn't enough to endear me to anyone. I just thought of the similarities in how she presented herself and the way I'd been in my dream.

In listening to her verbal assault, I was humbled as to the stoicism of the client. I recognised the parallels in what she was saying with what I'd said in my dream, for which I felt guilty, except my boss made my presentation look like a kindergarten parent/teacher interview. I'd never heard her be so brutal, not even to me. As ever, she was articulate and terse, but so vicious that the only respite in the receiving was in the words that had the translators struggling and humbly asking for a momentary pause to consult a dictionary or confer over the meaning of one of her obscure words.

It went on and on. Three hours of unbridled, pointed rhetoric which cut a swathe through the soul of everyone assembled. None of it was directed at me, but I felt for those in the firing line just the same. The first tear was met with some embarrassment from all of the customer group, but my boss seemed to take it as a sign that she'd met her mark and proceeded to focus her efforts further. No-one was allowed to leave and eventually sniffles and red eyes were evident on everyone who was able to prevent themselves from blubbering outwardly.

Aside from the way she delivered her observations, what she said was largely the same as my own fantasised presentation, yet we were worlds apart. Even at my worst in my dream I understood no-go zones, even though I'd considered myself devoid of decorum. I'd kept it professional, primarily for my want to not dilute the legitimacy of what I was saying. But my boss seemed to have no qualms about destroying these people professionally and personally. She attacked them for their attire, their looks, their parentage, their country of origin, their culture, their history, their everything. Only when she figured that they'd been suitably crushed inside did she even start to rip apart the fabric of their corporate roles.

I'm surprised they let it continue really. I'd borne the brunt of these kinds of outbursts regularly over the years but I'd been fortunate in that they rarely lasted longer than an hour. I'd settle myself into my happy place and listen vacantly, nodding and bowing my head occasionally to demonstrate my attentiveness and deep seated submission. When it was over, I'd typically trudge back to my desk and look for solace in those parts of my life that she'd spared. Sometimes just a few moments staring at the pictures of my family on my desk was enough to return a shallow smile to my defeated face and help me make it through the day. It was childish but I knew that smile would torment her. But there was no reprieve or end in sight for any of those assembled.

The air of the boardroom was thick with an acrid mix of fear, resentment and anger. When she did allow a five minute interval for them to compose themselves there was a rush for the door reminiscent of a schoolyard rush at home-time. I didn't follow them from the room, though I did partake of the fresher air nearer the door.

Left on our own, I expected my boss to just ignore me. She barely glanced my way throughout proceedings and I felt some relief that perhaps I was invisible to her. Until she spoke.

"Could you have done better than that, you prannock?" she asked.

"That depends on what your intention was," I said, oddly brave considering I'd just witnessed her in what would have been politely described in my company as being in 'classic' form. "Did you want to make a point or destroy them completely?"

She looked at me with bloodshot, penetrating eyes but with an almost post-coital smile. "Still want to resign?"

"Even more so," I volunteered with confidence. Now more than ever I didn't want to be a party to an organisation so willing to attack people with impunity. "Your effort has done nothing to convince me that I should stay or that I'd ever want to work with you again." There was pride in my voice and I subconsciously braced myself for her response accordingly, but she said nothing. I felt the seconds drag out while she sat caressing her hair. I couldn't stop the concern from rising in me.

"They'll be back in about three minute's time. They won't be late."

"And?"

"And when they return I'm going to share news of some changes at our company, particularly your advancement and that my presentation is in fact at your direction. Why else would I deliver such a poisoned challis?"

"Good luck with that," I said, nervously fumbling my phone in my pocket.

"I don't need luck. I've got a long history with these types of engagements and there's no way I'd commit such an act of professional suicide of my own undertaking." Her facial expression settled into one of arrogant contentment.

"You're my boss. They know it and they'll never buy into that fairy tale." I did my best to sound convincing but my confidence of abstraction was most definitely on the wane.

"What was it you said a moment ago?" she feigned a rhetorical pause. "Ah yes, 'good luck with that'."

"Why would you deliver my presentation if it was that abhorrent to you, let alone if you are my superior? Whatever way you look at it, that you didn't intervene will mean you'll be tainted in the same way."

"I can and will look after myself, I can assure you."

"So is this supposed to encourage me to stay?"

"What has that got to do with it? Chances are your tenure at my company or in this entire industry is about to be beyond salvaging."

There were no words to capture how I felt. My self-esteem flat-lined and I felt the colour drain from my skin and my soul. She was evil and I'd been beaten by her decisively. There was no coming back from this. I felt cheated by the world. The benevolent universe which had seen fit to grant me such understanding as it had in my dream was now about to destroy me. The universe which had allowed me an epiphany which I thought was meant to save me was in fact granting me only a pyrrhic victory, taunting me with insight that I'd never come to fully realise. I was beyond questioning why.

I fell back into my traditional submissive, placative demeanour which sometimes worked with her. "What now then?"

"Two minutes."

"What am I supposed to do before they get back?"

"Call your wife perhaps. I don't really know or care for whatever distracts you in your life."

"But what do I need to do to avert this?"

"Nothing."

"Is this your way of making me stay?" I asked, concerned to the point of despair.

"Why would I want to prevent that?"

No words came to me in reply. I felt too betrayed by both her and the universe to do anything. It was a punishing blow, but as in my dream it came with it's own resurgence of strength and understanding. I recognised immediately that this was a revelation unto itself, but not as I expected.

Chapter - 41.

I'd already accepted that I needed to move on and change jobs, that much was a given. Listening to her only reminded me that I'd still resigned and nothing she had said or could do would make me retract that resignation. But I now also understood that my dream was far more than a message for my personal development and was meant for more than just my benefit. Just as I'd benefitted from understanding my life, the universe was inviting me to participate in the betterment of society at large by addressing an unparalleled source of evil. This latest upwelling of hate in me had a purpose; it was intended to make me see that she couldn't be allowed to continue. It wasn't fair on anyone, myself included, that she should be allowed to live and it was up to me to do something about it. For the good of mankind, she had to die.

Particularly after what I'd dreamed, I didn't think I'd have it in me to kill someone but I'm only human. Perhaps I'd never really thought of it and maybe this was deliberate. My soul surely understood me better than my conscious self and prevented me from ever getting the time to drift into any thought which might turn vengeful. Now after watching her and witnessing the effects of her on others, the imaginings began and options cycled through me just as I'd dreamed.

I was still contemplating options when the procession of management started to file back into the room. A break in the savagery did not appear to metabolise any fortitude in them. They looked just as they had when they'd left except that everyone had freshly polished moist skin around their eyes, and their number had this time been bolstered by Emile. It was easy to convince myself of public interest when I saw the shattered faces of everyone she'd spoken at.

When everyone was seated, my boss mouthed some words which I first I didn't understand until she silently repeated herself. "Time's up."

Something occurred to me as I looked beyond the chastised eyes of the customer and wondered what they were thinking and in particular whether they were thinking as I was. I figured behind their facades of stoic professionalism would be turmoil that couldn't be suppressed forever. All it would take was for a chink in their emotional armour to be breached and there would be no telling as to what these people would be capable of. My altered perspective opened my eyes. *En masse* I'm sure to her we represented only a room full of meat for the slaughter, perhaps me more than the rest. But together we were something more, regardless of whether she saw or recognised it.

I tuned out to what she was saying. Committed on a purpose beyond self-interest I didn't even flinch when I heard my name mentioned occasionally. Instead, I reviewed the faces of everyone assembled, like a king looking to gauge the support or dissent in his subjects. Broken and defeated, I likened how they looked to what I saw in the mirror every single day. Maybe it was even worse for them in that they didn't have the benefit of being conditioned to expecting those extremes of professional abuse over a protracted period.

Emile had been spared until now, but now he bore the brunt of my boss's assault. His reaction to her was, however, different to everyone else who'd previously been subjected to her critique. He stood to receive whatever it was that my boss saw fit to turn into a weapon, but there was a clear strength in his bravery. With his double breasted tailored jacket buttoned, he thrust his chest out and with each salvo he even appeared to be more composed. The guy was absorbing the aggression in everything he was being met with and I was in awe.

I was witnessing a battle of good versus evil; my boss against Emile. My boss was beyond frustration that she couldn't bring the senior guy to his knees and she pulled out all stops. In contrast, Emile didn't lower himself to retaliate or even justify his managerial practice. He stood, smiling with the contentment of the moral high ground, but it wasn't natural. There was no way he could brave that onslaught without an end in sight.

Just as everyone has their breaking point, everyone clearly also has their coping strategy. My 'find a happy place and ignore it' approach had not been particularly effective and I was hardly going to advocate its' use to others. I'd also seen many of my colleagues over the years resign in what my boss would later describe as a 'run away and cry' response, but I'd never seen anyone physically strike back.

I always believed that retaliation was perhaps inevitable if ever, whenever, control was overwhelmed by desire. That I'd never done it myself was paramount to proof that no matter how flawed I was, professionally or personally, I always maintained enough control stop myself. Media reports of someone slipping over the edge too consolidated my theory that uncontrolled desire could have devastating results. It never occurred to me that control could also see to blood being spilled in a corporate environment.

I looked over Emile's people again and saw the halo effect of his presence. United in support for Emile and fused in their contempt for my boss, where previously they had been subjugated now they appeared resolute and fortified. My boss had met her match, albeit not in a single person, but a competitor just the same.

My boss had stopped talking. Perhaps she'd said all she wanted to say or it was an extended pause, I couldn't tell. Whatever the cause, she was clearly content that she'd achieved what she'd set out to do. She sauntered abound the boardroom and eased herself into an empty seat at the foot of the table directly opposite Emile and, co-incidentally most probably, next to me. "You might like to say something before your departure," she said, ambiguously directed at either Emile or myself or possibly both of us. Clearly she mistook the mood around her for defeat and I was euphoric for knowing different.

Sedition was in the air and it was sweet. It quickened my pulse and invigorated me more than I recall it did in my dream, and moreover it was obvious that my fervour was shared. I felt individually invincible and amongst others similarly unassailable. I felt obligated to stand but unwilling do so. In standing I would surely ruin the dynamic of the room; it was like a warm bath for my soul and I was too comfortable in it to want to do anything which might disturb the situation. But this was my time, just as I'd imagined. For the first time in my memory, words serialised themselves in my mind for me to focus against her. Years of submission, fear and persecution all manifested itself as a clarity like I'd never experienced before, surpassing what I'd even dreamt of.

I stood casually, buttoned my jacket and paced around the table to Emile. I rested my hands on each of his shoulders from behind paternally and coaxed him back into his seat, ambivalent to the disparity in our ages. I dug deep, spoke with passion and drew on epithets of inspirational leadership and heartfelt belief in the team assembled. There was nothing abusive or derogatory and certainly nothing directed at any of the people who'd been so derided and belittled by my boss.

For all the years of being the arrogant outsider, even in a limited capacity, I finally understood that they didn't need me. Who was I to step in, breach their corporate culture and then direct them to what may or may not have been best practice in line with doctrine? These were professionals playing the cards they'd been dealt. They knew their business, their people and their strengths better than I or anyone else could grasp in any short engagement. For the first time in my life I really understood the contradiction of my career and that I was ideologically opposed to focussing on short term economics to improve a company's balance sheet. It was wrong that under the direction of my boss I'd recommend restructures that would see to hundreds or thousands of people lose their jobs, particularly when I'd lived my life in fear of losing mine. I could no longer advocate for any layoffs which would only reduce their experience base and longer term capabilities. It wasn't right. Just as I had obligations to my family, these companies had obligations to their employees which extended beyond the short term gains espoused by my kind. My boss had no heart, no conscience and no idea of the sociological implications of every 'successful engagement' she'd completed, but I was different.

Far from being the harbinger of doom or negativity, I emphasised the positives in what I'd heard of their organisation and the future. It wasn't hard. I was free and not obligated to speak so as to upsell my continued engagement at this company as if their future depended on it. Technically, I therefore avoided the question of the purpose of my visit. That my boss had taken it upon herself to destroy these people had made our original agenda irrelevant anyway. Now what was important was that I tend to *my* agenda. I shared a different plan, one based on an updated revamp of the ideals of what was already a strong company but which had just lost its confidence in a fickle economic climate.

As I spoke, I walked slowly back to my boss, briefly resting my hand on the chair-back of as many of the team as was practical en route without making the action look laboured. I had their support without this little stunt, but it was a worthwhile show of strength. She sighed loudly and made to push her chair away from the table in order to stand, but I denied her the opportunity by using my foot to stop her chair from rolling backwards. She wasn't pleased, but I condescendingly patted her on the head like a dog just the same. It wasn't often that I'd seen her that furious and barely able to keep herself composed. She started to breathe noisily through her nose, almost snorting like a bull about to charge a fighter waving a red cape. I held her to the table until I thought she was going to hyperventilate herself into a coma.

I was going to start on her but I didn't. I had the words prepared, the audience primed, and my boss positioned such that she couldn't escape but I couldn't bring myself to do it. As righteous as I felt, I wasn't going to stoop to her level no matter how much I wanted to say what had been festering inside me for years.

Needless to say, I didn't think the client organisation bought into my boss's ruse. I felt their support, and their pity, but definitely not that my career was at an end like my boss had threatened. It dawned on me that I'd unwittingly identified a whole new niche of management consultancy, one where their employees and their companies won. I would be the only one willing to look beyond the immediate gains of losing those 'costs', seeing them instead as people.

I did another lap of the table with slow, confident but not quite arrogant steps. I'd said all that I wanted to say, now I just wanted to see what would happen. Had I been a gambling man I would have tried to put a little money on the likelihood of my boss talking. The only problem was that no bookmaker would have taken that bet; it was just too obvious. She was a seething mass of vitriol and resentment just waiting to begin and I couldn't believe that she'd held her tongue until now. Her fingernails had scratched tracts into the mahogany and her eyes were so bloodshot that any tears could have been bottled at the blood bank. She was irate. She stared me down for a time and then beckoned me to her side.

There was something hypnotic in the manner with which she summonsed me. One moment I was proud and confident, the next I sensed my life-force and strength being drained. By the time I was at her side I was weakened, but there was still some fortitude left in me. Where once I would have been a cowering wretch, now I found myself a mortal faced with an overwhelming but still fallible opponent.

A crow darted past the window at first then returned and came to a fluttery struggled hover immediately behind my boss. It was both poetic and poignant that a life-form so traditionally associated with death and malaise would appear at this time. Synonymous with evil and the devil, the bird appeared to be making a statement; it's mouth agape and presumably making quite a lot of noise that was not audible on our side of the glass. I wondered for a time if the bird heralded an omen and then if that warning was intended for my benefit or hers. My boss was unfazed or perhaps oblivious to the presence of the bird which did little to offset my bewilderment over the spectacle.

Then it happened. Emile stood, proud and true and bowed his head just enough for the gesture to be perceptible to his people, all of whom then too stood and did likewise, all without a word being spoken. Except that I could hear her breathing it was almost as if I was suddenly deaf; everyone was standing but saying nothing and the bird was flapping it's big black wings silently.

Her breathing quickened, her arms tensed and she leaned forward over the table. Time slowed and the universe granted me the heightened sensory awareness to either confront or enjoy what was to happen. I felt the flicker of incandescent lighting and the fluorescent lighting took the form of slow deliberate semaphore. I heard sweat and stress hormones ooze from her pores and chunks of cholesterol dislodge from her arteries and move like debris before a tsunami. Stress had never been so apparent and yet so glorious.

My mind braced itself for her to attack with the speed she'd demonstrated in my dream and I took a step back in anticipation, all the while marvelling that gravity was too slow for me to truly move in an earthly sense. Her temples pulsed and the irises of her eyes flashed with each slow surly heartbeat. Unlike in my dream, I was ready for her. Had she tried to shoot me I swear I could have dodged a bullet, but that seemed so unlikely. She was an advertisement for hypertension and as I watched her it was plausible that I might watch her experience a stroke.

Had time not been so slow, the way she pushed herself away from the table would have been seen as a thrust. Her arms and legs co-ordinated the strength necessary to roll her chair over my foot or something else which had previously blocked her movement, assuming that it was still there. But my foot had long since moved. I watched the alarm on her face as she realised the error she'd made and tried to compensate. I heard flicks of varnish on the mahogany be scraped off with her short functional fingernails, casually at first and then more desperately as the tips of her fingers passed the edge of the table. Then her arms started to flail looking for something else to grab, but there was nothing immediately behind her and no-one with the reflexes to intercept her.

She rolled backwards with such momentum that she showed no sign of slowing. Then something occurred to her. She turned her head and for a joyous microsecond her eyes looked in my direction, but they continued past me until she was looking clear over her shoulder. Then it occurred to me what was so obvious to her. Her chair was made of steel and she was hurtling towards a sheet of plate glass unlikely to withstand a collision.

I wondered what others saw. Perhaps their minds weren't double or even triple sampling life as mine was and they saw only a blur of motion faster than their brains could anticipate what would happen next. I saw the inevitability; that kinetic energy plus window was going to equal breakage.

With the impact came my turn to be unable to see what was going to happen. My synapses still fired like a Tesla experiment but I just couldn't see into the future. I watched the momentary relief on her eyes that she would finally be able to stand to say what she deemed so important, but she hadn't stopped moving yet. Her speed might have slowed marginally but not enough to see her come to a complete stop impeded only by a thin sheet of glass backed only by air. The glass conceded more than what seemed reasonable, bowing before finally fracturing with large cracks radiating from the point where the base of the chair struck. Perhaps the window would have been able to maintain its structural integrity with just the cracks, but not with a chaired adult continuing to push. Soon the movement was less against the window as through a cascade of sparkling fragments.

She wasn't moving fast enough to launch herself into oblivion, but soon gravity took over and lateral movement turned to a downward trajectory as her chair articulated on the edge. There was no teetering or remarkable balancing act. She was going down, physically not metaphorically and she knew it. She composed herself enough to accept her fate; I saw it in her eyes. There was resignation but without fear or disappointment. I hope she saw the heartfelt smile on my face. Top heavy as it was, the char upended itself as she fell away. The last I saw of her was the sole of her shoes.

Time returned to normal fluidity, emphasised by a volley of long absent ambient noise, a burst of cool breeze entering the room and the occasional chard of glass landing on parquet rather than disappearing down the side of the building. The crow continued its flapping hover for a time, unperturbed by the short-lived interruption to the air around it, then it too fell away. I fought to rationalise that it was more than likely only looking at its' reflection in the glass and wasn't anywhere near as prophetic as it appeared.

Elsewhere in the room there was silence and guarded facial expressions. Everyone was still standing by virtue of the fact that it had all happened so fast, but now that it was over everyone was at a loss as to what to do. I took a few slow paces to investigate her point of departure, peering over the edge cautiously from a distance. She wasn't coming back from this like in some 1950's Western where the hero implausibly and surreptitiously leaps to safety unbeknownst to everyone. A crowd was gathering on the street about 70 floors below us. I felt a weight lift from my shoulders.

Emile only needed to raise his head to reacquire everyone's attention. He took a deep breath and looked at me but spoke to his people. "This company has grown on the efforts of people who are prepared to stand tall in the face of adversity and in some cases even internal opposition. No better has this been illustrated than in what has transpired here today. Call it whatever you like, but good people and their conduct will always come to light." There were widespread nods of appreciative concurrence. I couldn't believe he left it at that but he did. No mention of my boss's tirade, her vindictive provocation or her attempt to attribute her efforts to me, much less her disappearance.

I struggled for what to say, searching for something appropriate and poignant and professional but no words came. In the end I only muttered what was loud and clear in my sub-conscious, "I'm glad that's over."

This seemed to be the cue that Emile was waiting for. "Your plans for our future. Are they achievable?" I wasn't as focussed as he wanted and he needed to repeat himself before I really was capable of responding. "Your plans, the constructive criticism you provided. Are they realistic?"

"My honest opinion? Stay the course. Don't buy into anything drastic like the rest of the world. Focus on short term pain not gain and be the one organisation with the capability to bounce back. Nothing lasts forever." I spoke from the heart. I meant it.

Emile addressed his team. He didn't speak in English and none of the translators suggested they were obligated to do or say anything so I made the assumption that Emile's words were not for me. It was time I left.

Chapter - 42.

I waited until I was back at my hotel before I rang home. I'd spent the walk oblivious to the crowds around me; just me in my head in my own little world. I thought of my role in my family and in the world. I was free, capable and it was up to me to make my life into whatever I wanted it be. I decided that I could have it all, but it just needed to start somewhere. I chose my family.

By the time I was ready to make the call I'd received phone-calls from both the CEO of my company wanting to confirm what he'd heard and Emile wanting me to work for him. I told the CEO the news, embellished a little to include the word 'sad'. He seemed to accept the story as unfortunate before moving on to discussion of a vacancy in management. I told him I'd think about it. Discussing anything with him at this time was not a priority.

Emile's offer wasn't particularly impressive except that he recognised that much of what I needed could be done by remote. "What separated you from your predecessors was your belief in balance. You couldn't possibly achieve this if you spent your entire time away from home," he said. He hinted at regrets in his life which I appreciated but didn't ask him to elaborate on. He was right and who was I to argue. I suggested I'd think about that too.

I got my wife on one of those rare moments when she was seated, the phone within reach and a fresh cup of coffee in her hand. She was relaxed and receptive to a distinct lack of stress in my voice. We spoke for over an hour; one of those conversations that happens in movies but never in reality. I told of my dream, my epiphanies and then of the demise of my boss. Most importantly, I shared what this meant to me and to us. We were exuberant with the future and I felt as if my life's purpose had been re-affirmed.

Suffice to say I was to be a traveller no more and I was happy about it.

The End.

ABOUT THE AUTHOR

Garrett is a forty something Australian novelist, and also a geek, husband, father, cub scout leader and struggling marathon runner. He grew up in Perth, Western Australia, and has been lucky enough to live in or visit most of Australia and much of the world. He now lives in Melbourne with his family. Not averse to change, thus far, he has been an Army officer, software consultant and author. But this is just the beginning. 'The Traveller' is his second novel.

BY THE SAME AUTHOR

Minions

Devlin Bennett's life is no longer in free-fall, but only because he's hit the bottom. What's worse, his notoriety is such that opportunities and friends are few and far between. Until a new job lands in his lap.

Benign and well-paid, the role and his new peers are unfazed with his history. It's the chance he's desperate for and his life is surely on the improve. But when he is warned anonymously to not join a list of deceased past employees, the job loses some of its lustre. Unable to walk away or ignore the warnings, he needs to understand whether he's been handed a lifeline or a death-sentence.

His concerns are shared by an ageing detective investigating the death of the latest employee. Together, they just might unravel the truth that lies amongst a newly bereaved woman, a Balkan sociopath, a battered performance artist, an elusive ex-employee and his enigmatic employer's reference to a 'greater good'. What they learn might benefit them both, and others.

Guilt is just a matter of how much you understand the bigger picture.

THE TRAVELLER

Thanks for reading. I hope you enjoyed it.

Garrett Addison

For more information on Garrett Addison and his books, see his
website: www.garrettaddison.com